RICHARD A. LUPOFF

◆

THE EMERALD CAT KILLER

Complete and Unabridged

LINFORD
Leicester

First published in Great Britain

First Linford Edition
published 2017

A catalogue record for this book is available
from the British Library.

ISBN 978–1–4448–3168–9

Published by
F. A. Thorpe (Publishing)
Anstey, Leicestershire

Set by Words & Graphics Ltd.
Anstey, Leicestershire
Printed and bound in Great Britain by
T. J. International Ltd., Padstow, Cornwall

This book is printed on acid-free paper

THE EMERALD CAT KILLER

A valuable cache of stolen comic books originally brought insurance investigator Hobart Lindsey and police officer Marvia Plum together. Their tumultuous relationship endured for seven years, then ended as Plum abandoned her career to return to the arms of an old flame, while Lindsey's duties carried him thousands of miles away. Now, after many years apart, the two are thrown together again by a series of crimes, beginning with the murder of an author of lurid private-eye paperback novels and the theft of his computer, containing his last unpublished book . . .

1

Red stopped in place, turned her face to the sky and shook her fist angrily. She shot a string of obscenities at God for doing this to her. Why had she let herself lose focus and wander into this yuppie-infested neighborhood, and why had that bastard in the sky sent this storm after her?

She wore a ragged T-shirt and jeans and a pair of old sneakers with holes in the bottoms. She'd worn a hat earlier tonight — at least she thought she had — but that was gone, probably swept away by a gust of wind when she was thinking of something else. At least her hands were protected from the worst of the cold. There was an elementary school just up the street — she ought to know that, she'd been a student there once upon a time — and some kid must have dropped a pair of gloves on her way home from kindergarten or first grade or second grade, because Red had found them on the sidewalk and managed to pull them onto her skinny, undersized hands.

The rain was coming down, and there were even rumbles of thunder and flashes of lightning — not common with Pacific storms, but who the hell knew what God was going to do? She paused under a streetlamp to look down at herself. She was skinny, the skinniest she could ever remember being. The cold rain and wind made her nipples stick out through the thin shirt. At least that was one good thing. They might attract the attention of a john, if there was such a thing as a john in this neighborhood full of smug householders and students from smug families.

And the fuzz patrolled this neighborhood. She knew that. It was too late at night for panhandling. Nothing to shoplift; all the stores would have turned off their lights and closed up before now.

It was her own fault. Bobby had told her to stay in the flatlands when he turned her out for the night's work. Stay in the Berkeley flatlands, or better yet, head for West Oakland. There was more business there, and the cops were more likely to look the other way as long as what was going on involved what they called consenting adults.

Was she a consenting adult? How old was she? Hard to remember her last birthday. Hard to remember anything anymore. Turned out in high school, dropped out, busted, released, juvenile hall, released, using, hooking, dealing. If she hadn't found Bobby — or if Bobby hadn't found her — there was no telling where she would be by now. Maybe dead.

Although that didn't sound like such a bad idea, either.

A flash of lightning showed her a black-and-white coming up Claremont from the direction of Oakland. She was pretty sure she was still on the Berkeley side of the city line, but cops from both cities liked to cruise in this neighborhood, crisscrossing the boundary with impunity.

She ducked behind a parked car. The black-and-white swept by, its tires making a hissing sound on the rain-wet roadway. She didn't want to get picked up now.

She needed a jolt and she didn't care how she got it — from a pill, a snort, or a pipe. She liked the pills best. They were like jellybeans — fun and easy to take. She'd tried a pipe, and it burned her throat and made her cough. And she was seriously afraid of needles.

Man, was she ever cold. If only she could get inside somewhere, out of this rain. She contemplated checking out the backyards of some of the houses in this neighborhood. Maybe she could sneak into a garage or a basement and get dry. She'd even try a kid's playhouse or a storage shed.

The black-and-white was gone. She hoisted herself to her feet, using the door handle of a shiny new sedan. She caught a glimpse of herself in the car's window. Oh man, what a vision. No wonder the johns were so few these days. She looked like a hag of forty, maybe even older. Nobody would take her for . . . She tried to remember her actual age. Her hair was dirty and ragged, she'd lost half her teeth, and her complexion looked like an old soccer ball.

Maybe she could find a junkie looking for a fix. She could steer him to Bobby, and Bobby would make a sale and let her stay in the room overnight and not have to hit the street again.

Fat chance.

She started down the street again, trying car doors. They were all locked. She caught another glimpse of herself in a window. Yes, her hair was red. That must be why her name was Red. Or maybe Rita, Rhoda, something like that. It was just so hard to remember anything, to think about anything except getting a jolt. Getting a jellybean or two. Getting dry and getting a jolt.

Another black-and-white rolled past, and she ducked behind another car until it disappeared into the darkness and the rain. A gust of wind threw a piece of flying cardboard against her, and she had to peel it off her back and toss it into the middle of the street, screaming at God to give her a place to sleep, out of the storm. At least that.

Her face was wet, and she couldn't tell whether it was with rain or tears.

She'd better get off the main drag. Too many black-and-whites; too much chance of getting dragged down to the lockup on MLK.

She turned down a little side street. Most of the lights were off. Smug burghers were nestled all snug in their beds while visions of . . . what? She couldn't remember. Visions of something danced in their heads. Visions of jellybeans, maybe.

Holy cow, an unlocked car! She pulled open the door, crawled in, shut the door behind her. Oh, all right, dry and warm and safe. If only she had a jolt, life would be perfect right here in her own little nest of safety. She slid across the seat, reached up and turned the rear-view mirror so she could see herself, at least a little, in the small light that was available.

One look and she started to cry again. She'd been a pretty girl. Her parents had loved her, her father especially. Her mother was so self-absorbed, Red sometimes wondered if the old broad even remembered having her. She was popular with her schoolmates. And boys. Boys really liked her.

When had she lost it? She couldn't remember. It didn't matter. Red, that's who she was. Or Rhonda. Or Robbie. Was she Robbie? No, that was Bobby. Bobby was her source. Bobby loved her, or he would someday. So she wasn't Robbie. Maybe Rosie. Little Red Rosie, wasn't that a nursery rhyme? Something like that.

She looked around inside the car. Maybe there was something here worth ripping off. They said you could get some nice money for a good car stereo, but she didn't know how to get one out of a car; and if she did, how would she get it back to Bobby's room in the old Van Buren Hotel down on Acton Street? No, that wouldn't work.

She punched open the glove compartment and pulled out a fat wad of papers. Maps, owner's manuals, insurance certificates, registration papers. Christ, this guy must never throw anything away. She pawed around the dashboard until she found a knob that she recognized as a cigar lighter. Imagine, everybody used to have these things in their cars. She punched it, waited till it popped back out, pulled it out of its little hole and stared at the glowing bull's-eye of red-hot wires. She held it up to her face so she could feel the warmth. It was really great. She decided to warm herself, pushed it against her cheek, and screamed when she felt the burning, searing heat on her skin.

She dropped the lighter. It bounced off something hard lying on the floor. She reached down to see what it was. Something black, almost like an attaché case only not an attache case, more like — she almost had it, she'd get it in a minute — but somebody in the house must have heard her scream. She saw a light come on in the house; heard a little yippy dog sending up an alarm.

Somebody was going to come and grab her, she knew it. If she could get out of the car fast enough and get away, she'd be all right. Or maybe she should lock the car door. She should have done that in the first place, but she didn't think of it; she was too occupied with getting warm and dry and swallowing jellybeans. She started to get out of the car, then realized what the black thing was; realized that she'd hit paydirt after all.

Her heart beat wildly and her blood sang in her veins. This was something she could sell for real money. Or she could bring it to Bobby and he could sell it, and they'd share the money. He'd let her stay with him in his room on Acton Street. She wouldn't even need any of the money. He could have it all. She'd take out her share in jolts.

Some ancient guy wearing pyjamas and a bathrobe must have come out of the house because he was pulling at the car door. He got it open and reached for her but she didn't wait for him to grab her. She could have scrambled out the other side of the car, but this was too exciting. She screamed at the guy and jumped out of the car, straight at him.

He was startled. He hadn't expected that, the sucker hadn't. She'd never seen anybody look so surprised. He actually backed away from her. There was a brick thingamabob behind him, a plinth or a pilaster or whatever the hell they called them in art history class. She laughed at him. She went for him; the black thing in her hands was a laptop computer and those things were worth real money, worth even more than car radios or cell phones.

The sucker saw her coming at him and he threw up his hands. She hit him smack on with everything she had, smashed him in the face with the laptop computer.

There were more lights on in the house and the little yippy dog was going absolutely bonkers nuts.

The guy she'd hit lurched backward, his head jerking backward against the brick thingamabob, and then the front door of the house opened and the little yippy dog came swarming at her, followed by a dumpy old broad waving her arms. Red split; she turned around and she ran, ran back to the bigger street, turned, and ran, and ran, and ran, the laptop computer hugged to her chest, her feet soaked with icy rainwater that came up through the holes in her sneakers. She was screaming, 'Bobby, Bobby, open up, Bobby, let me in, Bobby, Bobby, I've got something for you, Bobby, for us, Bobby, something wonderful. Oh, love me, Bobby, love me.'

2

One year later . . .

'Lindsey?'

It only took one word to make the old synapses kick back in. If he'd been a retired soldier he'd have wanted to jump out of bed and stand at attention. If he'd been a retired fire horse he'd have snorted once, shaken himself, and been ready to pull the wagon to the conflagration.

Hobart Lindsey grunted, 'Yes, Mr. Richelieu.'

He pressed the phone to his ear, swung himself around, and planted his feet in his fleece slippers. How long had he been retired? He'd put in enough years at International Surety to qualify for his pension. He wasn't eligible for Social Security yet and the monthly checks from I.S. weren't exactly lavish, but he'd been able to keep the little house in Walnut Creek after his mother remarried and moved to Oceanside Villas, a gated retirement community in Carlsbad.

He waited to hear what Desmond Richelieu, his old chief at International Surety, top executive at Special Projects Unit / Detached Service, would be calling him about at this hour of the morning. In fact . . . Lindsey frowned, peered at the glowing readout on his bedside clock, and waited for Richelieu to say what he had to say.

'Lindsey, I need you back on board.'

'I'm retired, Mr. Richelieu.' He couldn't bring himself to call his old chief Ducky, the name that everyone used when Richelieu was out of earshot.

'I know that. You get a fat check every month for not working.'

'Mr. Richelieu, I earned it.'

'All right, look — wait a minute, where the hell are you, Lindsey?'

'Don't you know? You called me. I'm at home.'

'Yeah, yeah, vegetating. I'm still working, why aren't you?'

Lindsey didn't even try to answer that; didn't bother to remind Richelieu that he'd been downsized out of his job and forced into early retirement. 'Look, Chief,' he said, 'I'm sure you called me for a reason. You realize it's an hour earlier here in California than it is there in Denver? Did you just want to wake me up, or is there some ulterior motive?'

'You're getting feisty in your old age, Lindsey.'

'Yep.' He stretched, stood up, and started toward the kitchen. Thanks be given for cordless telephones!

'You were always the go-to guy on wacko cases. I've got your file right here on my monitor. Comic books, that Duesenberg with the solid platinum engine, Julius Caesar's toy chariot. You were always the oddball. Maybe that's why you were so good at the loony cases.'

'Thanks, Chief. You should have said that at my retirement banquet when they gave me the gold wristwatch and the fond farewell. Oh, wait a minute, I didn't get a retirement banquet, gold wristwatch, or fond farewell. I got a fond *Don't-let-the-door-hit-you-on-the-way-out*. Look, I am longing for a cup of coffee and a plate of scrambled eggs, and since there's nobody here to make them, I need to get off the phone and do it myself. Unless there's something you want.'

'You know about the consulting fee account.'

'Right.'

'I can offer you some nice bucks for a few hours of easy work.'

'Right. And there's a really nice bridge you'd like to sell me.'

'No, I mean it.'

'Okay, hold on.' He laid the phone on the counter, turned on the coffee maker, got a couple of eggs out of the fridge and set them where he could keep a watchful eye on them, then plopped himself into a kitchen chair.

Desmond Richelieu's voice came squirming out of the telephone. 'Are you there? Are you there? Damn you, Lindsey, where the hell did you go?'

Lindsey picked up the phone. 'Sorry 'bout that, Chief. Now, what were you saying?'

'You ever hear of Gordon Simmons, Lindsey?'

Lindsey frowned. 'I don't think so.'

'You don't keep up with things, do you?'

'Chief, please. He's not related to Flash Gordon on the Planet Mongo, is he? I've always had a fondness for old Buster Crabbe.'

'Don't joke, you. Listen, don't take it for granted that your pension is guaranteed, Lindsey. Don't get me peeved.'

'Chief, it *is* guaranteed. Who's Gordon Simmons?'

'Not is. Was. He died a year ago. Murdered.'

'Sorry, Chief. You want to tell me more, or let me scramble my eggs? I'm hungry this morning.' He looked out the kitchen window. Beyond gauzy, pale blue curtains, the sky was a vivid shade, almost cobalt, and the sun was bright. 'Did we cover the decedent? Is there a problem with the claim? Why is this a case for SPUDS? I'm sorry Mr. Simmons was murdered, but why are you calling me about it? Especially a year after his death.'

'It's not about the death claim. We paid that off. No problem.'

Lindsey sighed. 'Can I call you back after I've had my breakfast?'

'No, damn it, no! I don't give a damn about your breakfast. Now listen. The guy lived in Berkeley. Simmons. He had a policy with us. Beneficiary was his wife. Walnut Creek office handled the claim. They paid the claim and we closed the case. This is a new case.'

'You'll have to enlighten me, Chief.'

'We've got a potential lawsuit on our hands. Mrs. Simmons is threatening to sue a publisher called Gordian House. It's a plagiarism suit. She has a co-plaintiff, a publisher called Marston and Morse. Gordian House has kicked it over to us. If the case gets to court and they lose, we have to pony up. And the Widder Simmons and M-and-M want big bucks. Big bucks, Lindsey.

'Here's what I want you to do. The case file is on the SPUDS server. Get into the Walnut Creek office and read through it. Nobody there has enough brains for this case. Just read the file and call me back and tell me you'll handle this one.'

Lindsey poured himself a cup of coffee,

then added some half-and-half. He didn't say anything.

There was a lengthy silence. He could hear Richelieu breathing and knew he was waiting for him to say he'd take the case. Lindsey was determined to outwait his one-time boss. After all, it was the company's dime, not Lindsey's.

Finally, Desmond Richelieu said, 'Please.'

It was the first time Lindsey had ever heard him say that word. True, Lindsey could tell, even from the distance of a thousand miles, that Richelieu said it through clenched teeth and very nearly with tears in his eyes. Still, he said it.

To Lindsey, that constituted an offer he couldn't refuse.

★   ★   ★

The Walnut Creek office of International Surety occupied a suite in a modern high-rise building across North Main Street from city hall. Lindsey left his Dodge Avenger in the parking garage beneath the office building. He liked everything about the car, especially its safety features, except for the name. Why name a car after a World War II torpedo bomber?

He rode up in an elevator full of hard strivers half his age. The receptionist at International Surety looked up from her monitor screen and stared at him as if she feared that he would die on the spot of superannuation.

Lindsey said, 'I'm from SPUDS. Need to talk with the branch manager about the Simmons case.'

The woman hit a buzzer on her desk and Elmer Mueller emerged from somewhere. He'd gained weight and lost hair since Lindsey had seen him last. And how long had that been? Lindsey wondered.

Elmer Mueller offered a reluctant handshake and ushered Lindsey into his private office. Behind Mueller's desk and across North Main, city hall gleamed in the March sunlight. Mueller gestured Lindsey to a chair.

The decor was modern. Elmer Mueller's desktop was clear except for a keyboard and monitor. That seemed to be the standard of the day. But the portraits on Mueller's wall were of President

Richard Nixon and Governor Pat Brown. Lindsey wondered if Mueller's intention was ironic.

'Richelieu e-mailed me about you, Lindsey.' Elmer Mueller leaned back in an overstuffed leather chair. He swiveled, nodded permission to city hall to stay where it was, then swung back toward Lindsey. 'We've had to cut back. I can't spare people to hold your hand, and I don't like SPUDS poking its nose into my business.'

'Your business?' Lindsey raised his eyebrows.

'Running this branch. If Ducky has any complaints about the way I run this office, he can file a beef with corporate.' He dropped a fist onto the sheet of gray-tinted glass that topped his desk. 'How long since you worked out of this office, Lindsey?'

Lindsey smiled. 'Twenty-two years, Elmer.'

'Didn't I see your name in the retirement column of *IntSurNews* a few years ago?'

'Ducky asked me to come back on

special assignment.'

Mueller pursed his lips like an exasperated schoolteacher and swung his head slowly from side to side. 'I suppose I might as well set you up. There's an empty office in the suite. Remember Mrs. Blomquist?'

Lindsey said that he did.

'Dropped dead. Had her retirement papers in, bought a condo down in La Jolla, had her furniture shipped ahead. Moved into a motel for her last few days in Walnut Creek. Came in to clean out her desk and say goodbye, and dropped dead. You can use her computer.'

Lindsey thanked him. The receptionist showed him to the vacant office and handed him a printout of file access codes. She closed the door behind her. Lindsey got to work.

The computer file on the Simmons case was sparse. Policy date and number, premium payment records, date of death, cause of death, coroner's and police reports, claim forms and record of payment to beneficiary. Everything looked normal. Lindsey felt sorry for Simmons's widow,

Angela. He wondered if there were any children. If so, they weren't listed on the policy. But it had been in effect for a long time. Maybe Simmons took it when the couple were newlyweds and never added bennies when the tykes came along. Bad work by the agent, if that was so.

He printed out what he needed, checked the beneficiary's phone number, and placed a call to Mrs. Simmons. A neutral voice answered, 'Rockridge Savings and Loan. If you know your party's extension, enter it now. Otherwise, please speak the name of your party and stay on the line for assistance. This call may be recorded or monitored for quality control.'

'Mrs. Simmons, please.'

She had a pleasant enough voice. She didn't sound particularly grief-stricken, and obviously she'd returned to work. But then it had been a year since Gordon Simmons's demise.

Lindsey explained that he was investigating Simmons's death in connection with the lawsuit. Mrs. Simmons said that she got off work at four o'clock and

Lindsey arranged to come to her home.

Before he took his leave of the branch office, he returned Richelieu's earlier call. 'Okay, got it, Mr. Richelieu.' Oh, how he longed to call him Ducky to his face — or to him over the telephone. Maybe someday. Maybe not. 'Okay,' he continued, 'you know that our client is looking at a nasty copyright infringement suit. We already paid a death claim related to this case, and now we're on the other side of the fence.'

'For heaven's sake, Lindsey, tell me something I don't know.'

'Who's our lawyer? Shouldn't that information be in the file?'

'Isn't it there? You'll be happy about that one, at least. You remember your old buddy Eric Coffman?'

'Of course I do.'

'Well he didn't put in his retirement papers and go home to sit on his hindquarters and collect pay for no work. He's still earning his keep. And he's our sheriff on this one if we can't head the rustlers off at the pass.'

'He doesn't work for I.S., does he?'

'He's on retainer.'

'Okay, at least that's good. I think I'll round up a posse and get a feel for what's going on before I call Eric. But if you feel like it, Mr. Richelieu, you send him a smoke signal to let him know I'm on the trail.'

And where the hell did all the cowboy talk come from?

★   ★   ★

The Simmons home was a comfortable-looking craftsman bungalow on Eton Avenue, a short side street not far from Rockridge Savings and Loan. A ten-year-old gray Chevy stood in the driveway. A shoulder-high brick pillar set off concrete steps leading to a heavy wood and cut-glass door. The house looked like Depression-era construction, well kept, with a tidy front lawn and a small, carefully tended flower bed.

Lindsey had parked at the curb. He rang the doorbell and was greeted by a yipping dog.

Mrs. Simmons — her looks matched

the voice on the telephone to perfection — opened the door a crack and said, 'Mr. Lindsey?'

Lindsey passed a business card through the opening. It read, *International Surety / Special Projects Unit — Detached Service*. There was a cartoon image of a potato, the visual pun for SPUDS, and Lindsey's name.

'I hope you don't mind Millicent.' The woman pushed the dog aside and admitted Lindsey. Millicent sniffed his trousers, decided he was not a burglar, and backed away.

Moments later, seated in the living room, Lindsey said, 'Mrs. Simmons, I understand that you are suing Gordian House.'

'Angela, please. Angela Simmons. Marston and Morse and I. We haven't filed suit yet. We're contemplating it.'

Lindsey found himself liking her. She was casually but neatly dressed, her medium brown hair done in a soft style, her manner relaxed. This was a woman who knew who she was, who lived comfortably, if modestly, who accepted herself on her own terms and the world on its.

He said, 'Yes.'

'Gordon's publishers.'

'I'm sorry, I don't recognize his byline, 'by Gordon Simmons.' I'm afraid I don't read as much as I ought to.'

'That's all right, he didn't use his real name. I've saved copies of all his books. He was careless about them but I was proud of him. I saved all his editions.'

She crossed the room to a bookcase and returned carrying half a dozen paperbacks, which she spread on the coffee table. The covers featured colorful paintings and splashy lettering. The titles followed a pattern: *The Blue Gazelle, The Pink Elephant, The Yellow Thrush, The White Bat, The Purple Cow.*

Lindsey couldn't keep from starting to recite, 'I've never seen a purple cow . . . '

Angela put up her hand like a traffic cop stopping the flow of cars. 'We laughed about that a lot. Nobody younger than forty seemed to get the joke.'

Lindsey scanned the book covers. The artwork wasn't really bad. His own father had been a cartoonist and Lindsey had an eye for skillful rendering. The subject matter on these was fairly lurid, standard tough-guy-and-sexy-dame images. The byline was Wallace Thompson.

Lindsey looked a question at Angela Simmons.

'Gordon had a civil service job. There were government regulations about publishing outside work. I don't know what they were afraid of. Maybe that somebody would give away the secret codes of the social security system. Or maybe some little bureaucrat would write dirty books on the side and a politician would find out about it and kick up a fuss; accuse Uncle Sam of employing a pornographer. But it wasn't a bad thing. Gordon liked to keep his day job and his writing separate anyway. No one at the office knew about Wallace Thompson.'

Lindsey reached inside his jacket for a notebook and a silver International Surety pen. He hadn't got a gold watch, but at least he was given a silver pen and pencil when he said good-bye.

'You don't mind if I take a few notes?'

She didn't mind. In fact she offered to get them coffee, and Lindsey accepted with gratitude.

'Mr. Lindsey — '

'Hobart.'

'I don't understand why International Surety is involved. There's no problem with Gordon's life insurance, is there? You can't take the money back. It's all gone. I used it to pay off the mortgage on this house.'

Lindsey shook his head. 'Nothing like that. You see, International Surety isn't just a life insurance company. We sell many kinds of insurance, including business and indemnity policies.'

She waited for him to continue.

'We have an indemnity policy with Gordian House. If your suit against them — yours and Marston and Morse's — is successful, we'll have to reimburse Gordian House for their damages. The damages they will have paid. Do you see?'

'Then you're — ' Angela Simmons lowered her coffee cup onto its saucer with a clatter. 'Are you here — you're on their side? On Gordian's side? Mr.

Lindsey, I probably shouldn't be talking to you. At least not without my lawyer present. I think maybe you'd better leave. Right now.'

Lindsey slid his pen back into his pocket and closed his notebook. 'I'm not on anybody's side, Mrs. Simmons.' So much for Angela and Hobart. 'I'm just trying to understand the case.'

Mrs. Simmons stood, called Millicent, clicked a leash onto her collar, and walked to the door with Lindsey.

'Millicent needs to go out.'

At the bottom of the steps she stopped to let the dog sniff a bush. Apparently someone else had been there and left a message.

Angela Simmons laid her free hand on top of the brick pillar. 'It was right there,' she said.

Lindsey said, 'What do you mean?'

'Where Gordon hit his head.'

Lindsey waited.

'It was raining. We were in bed. Millicent started howling and woke us up.'

Apparently she had changed her mind

about talking to Lindsey. A minute ago she'd regarded him as the enemy. Now she was telling him the story of her husband's death.

'Gordon always locked the car. Not just at night. Even during the day, any time he wasn't driving, he always locked the car.'

She let out a deep breath.

'But he'd been working late at the library. He'd just finished a book. He hadn't even turned it in to his editor at Marston and Morse. He was starting research on the next one; that was why he had the laptop at the library. He came home with an armload of books, but it was dark out and it was raining hard and he couldn't handle everything at once. He brought the books into the house. He was so tired. He'd worked all day shuffling papers for the government and spent hours doing research at the library. He stayed until they closed. Once he was in the house he forgot all about his laptop. I made him a hot bowl of soup and a slice of toast. He was too tired to eat anything else. And then we went to bed.'

Millicent was tugging at her leash but

Angela Simmons was reliving that night a year in the past. 'When Millicent heard something — she *must* have heard something — she woke us and I said, 'Gordon, it's a burglar.' He put on his slippers and went downstairs but there was nobody there. I kept Millicent with me. I was afraid; I was holding her in bed. I heard the front door; Gordon went outside. Then I heard his voice but I couldn't make out what he said. Then I heard the car door open and Gordon's voice again, and then the car door slammed shut. I put Millicent's leash on her and we ran downstairs and outside. Gordon was lying on the ground.'

She gestured to the sharply pointed corner of the brick pillar. 'That was where it happened. I ran back in the house and called nine-one-one and the police came and an ambulance. Gordon's nose was broken; it was bleeding, and there was blood on the bricks here, too. I thought it was just his face — I thought he would recover, but they said that he'd smashed the back of his head on the corner of the bricks. He had bone splinters in his brain.' She stopped. She was out of breath. Millicent had got tired of waiting for her walk and done her business on the lawn.

Lindsey said, 'I'm sorry, Mrs. Simmons.' He couldn't think of anything else to say.

'They took him to the hospital. They tried to save him, but it was no use. He had splinters in his brain.' She blinked as if she'd fallen into the past for a moment, and then bounced back to the present. 'It must have been some homeless person. Probably some homeless man, maybe a woman — you can never tell nowadays.' Angela Simmons reached into her pocket and pulled out a plastic bag and a couple of paper towels. She cleaned up after Millicent, walked to a gray trash container, and dropped the bag into it. Then she came back and resumed her account. She'd caught her breath.

'It must have been some homeless person,' she repeated. 'It was raining and he must have been trying every car door he came to, looking for a place to sleep. At least that's what the police thought.

That's what they told me. Gordon always locked the car, but it was cold and raining, and he was so tired he forgot. Just that once, he forgot. The homeless man saw Gordon's laptop and he thought he could steal it and maybe sell it the next day. But Millicent heard him and Gordon went to investigate.'

Lindsey stood, listening. He could make his notes later. When an interviewee was on a roll, you just listened and remembered.

'The police thought that Gordon pulled open the car door to send the man away, and he smacked him in the face with the laptop. It must have been a man; a woman wouldn't do that, do you think? I think it must have been a man. He smashed him in the face with the laptop and knocked him back against the pillar. That's why his nose was broken and why he had bone splinters in his brain. That's why he's dead.'

'The killer was never found?' Lindsey asked. 'I would think — well, weren't there fingerprints in the car that could lead to the killer?'

Angela Simmons shook her head.

'But if the person was in the car — did he wipe off his fingerprints?'

'The police don't think so. They checked out the car and found plenty of prints — Gordon's, mine, some friend's that we gave a ride to the airport a week or so before. Everything was normal. But nothing that helped very much. I mean, nothing that helped at all, in fact. Nothing that helped at all.'

Lindsey started to take his leave, but she put her fingers on his wrist and detained him for another minute. 'They found an organ donor card in Gordon's wallet. I never knew about that. He wanted to donate his organs, and they took them at the hospital. Harvested them. That's what they call it, you know. They harvested his organs, and his heart is beating in another person's chest right this very minute. And somebody has his liver. And his spleen, and his pancreas. Even his eyeballs. They weren't damaged when he was hit. They use everything today; nothing goes to waste.'

Lindsey said, 'Like the Shmoo.'

Angela Simmons tilted her head and gave him a curious look. 'Like the what?'

'Nothing. Nobody remembers the Shmoo.' He managed a smile. 'A comic-strip creature that was so eager to be useful, it would just keel over when you looked at it. The bristles made toothbrushes, the eyes made buttons. The meat tasted like chicken.'

3

The Berkeley Police Department had gotten its new headquarters building at last. After the creaky old structure on McKinley Avenue, the nearby replacement looked modern and efficient from the outside. From the inside it resembled a medieval dungeon. Well, progress was progress.

Lindsey had phoned ahead, and he was met by a uniformed sergeant who could have passed for a shaving-lotion model, if there were such things anymore. Blond, blue-eyed, clean-shaven, and wearing a uniform that must have been custom-fitted, he looked like a private eye from a Richard Prather paperback, suddenly drafted into the official police force.

'Olaf Strombeck,' the shaving-lotion model introduced himself. They shook hands, exchanged business cards, and proceeded to Strombeck's office, Lindsey now wearing a visitor's badge on his jacket pocket.

Strombeck had pulled a file and laid it on his desk, but before opening it he said, 'Mr. Lindsey, I don't understand why you're here, sir. This is a police matter. This is an open case. I'm not sure just how much information I can give you.' He put his hand, palm down, on top of the file folder.

Lindsey nodded. 'Candidly, I'm just getting started on this. International Surety held a life policy on Mr. Simmons. We paid his widow. As far as we're concerned, that aspect of the case is over.'

'Then . . . what?'

'There's a threatened lawsuit — Mrs. Simmons and the Marston and Morse Publishing Company against Gordian House. International Surety has an indemnity policy with Gordian, and I'm gathering information to help us deal with that.'

'I don't get it.' Strombeck stood up. His uniform was severe: midnight-blue shirt, polished badge, a little enamel rectangle that Lindsey recognized as the Medal of Valor. Those didn't come easy, and in his experience officers who received them seldom cared to talk about the reason.

'I'm afraid this is getting close to a cold case. It's been a year. The official line, of course, is that we never close a homicide case until we've solved it. But it's also true that most murders are resolved quickly. And most of them are pretty straightforward. Domestic violence cases that get out of hand, vehicular homicides. Take away those two and we'd be down to a small fraction of our caseload. There are gang killings and holdups that go wrong. If you're ever threatened, Mr. Lindsey, give the bad guy your wallet. It isn't worth your life.'

'I learned that lesson long ago,' Lindsey said.

Strombeck resumed, 'The longer a case goes unsolved, the less likely it is that we'll find the perpetrator. And after a year, unless we catch a break through a DNA sample or — well, never mind the 'or'. I'm afraid the clearance rate on older homicides is not very good.'

'I understand, yes. Even so, I think these two cases are one, Sergeant.'

Strombeck lifted blond eyebrows, then nodded encouragingly.

'I've been talking with Mrs. Simmons.'

'Be careful, Mr. Lindsey.' Strombeck was suddenly serious, more serious than he had been. 'You're treading on dangerous ground. This is still a police matter.' He paused. 'And you are not a licensed investigator anyway, are you?'

Lindsey shook his head. 'I'm an insurance adjuster. Or was. Thought I had a great career going until I got downsized into early retirement.'

Strombeck did a magic trick and made Lindsey's business card reappear in his hand. 'I don't see 'retired' anywhere on this.'

'Old card.'

The eyebrows and the encouraging nod again.

'I'm too young for social security. It's nice to be too young for anything these days. I get a modest pension from International Surety. In return for that they pull me back in every now and then as a kind of superannuated temp. That's why I'm working this case.'

'Okay, that's good. But what does a squabble between two publishers — what were their names again?'

Lindsey told him. Strombeck jotted a note. 'Marston and Morse, Gordian House. I've heard of them both.'

'I wouldn't peg you as a literary man,' Lindsey said, smiling. 'Is it true that every police officer has a novel in his desk drawer?'

'Not so. You've been watching too many Barney Miller reruns.'

'Simmons wrote paperbacks for Marston and Morse,' Lindsey said. 'Under a pseudonym. Had to do that to stay out of trouble at his day job. They all had the same hero, a private eye named . . . ' He reached for his pocket organizer and flipped pages until he found what he wanted. ' . . . private eye named Tony Clydesdale. All the books had the same pattern for their titles. Named for animals. *Blue Gazelle, Pink Elephant*, like that.'

'I've heard of that. Didn't MacDonald use colors? And that Grafton woman uses the alphabet?'

This guy *must* be a reader! 'That's right.'

'So — I'm still looking for a connection, Mr. Lindsey.'

'So this other company, Gordian House, brought out a book with a similar title. *The Emerald Cat*. Different hero, if you can call him that, different byline. But Mrs. Simmons says that it was her husband's last book, somebody just went over it and changed a few names and sold it to Gordian. Gordon Simmons's laptop computer disappeared the night he was murdered. His wife thinks there was an unpublished novel in the computer.'

Lindsey drew a breath.

'Do you see where I'm going with this?'

'Ahah, the plot thickens,' Strombeck said. 'But this sounds like a plagiarism case. I'm not an attorney, you understand, but all cops have to be at least jack-lawyers, and I don't see any crime here. Sounds like a civil matter.'

Lindsey put away his pocket organizer. 'That may be so. But I remember something Lieutenant Yamura used to say. Is she still on the force, Sergeant?'

Strombeck grinned. Apparently he was fond of Dorothy Yamura. 'She's a captain now. Fine cop.'

''I'm sure that coincidences really

happen, but they make me nervous,''
Lindsey quoted. 'That's what Yamura
liked to say.'

Strombeck smiled and nodded. 'That's
Dorothy all right!'

'The Berkeley Police Department was
very helpful to me in resolving several
cases, and I like to think I helped the
police as well.'

Strombeck grunted encouragingly.

Lindsey said, 'And another officer.
Marvia Plum. Sergeant Plum.' Oh, butter
wouldn't melt in his mouth. If Strombeck
had X-ray vision he'd see Lindsey
quivering inside when he spoke the name.
How long had it been since he'd last
worked with Marvia, last seen her, last
touched her? But he managed to ask
about her as if it were a passing thought.

Strombeck paused, then shook his
head. 'Sorry, doesn't ring a bell. This is a
small police force, Mr. Lindsey. Everybody knows everybody. Berkeley isn't
exactly Mayberry R.F.D., but we're small
enough. Maybe Sergeant Plum is on the
University of California force. They're
about as big as we are.'

'I don't think so.'

'Well, maybe Oakland or Emeryville. Or Alameda County Sheriff?' Strombeck sounded like a man trying to be helpful, or at least sound helpful when he knew he wasn't really offering anything.

Lindsey said, 'I can see I have a lot of work to do. Thank you for your time, Sergeant Strombeck.'

'Any time, sir.'

'I'll take you up on that, Sergeant.' Lindsey pushed back his chair, stood up, and turned toward the doorway.

Strombeck said, 'Remember, sir, you stick to that insurance claim. Stay out of homicide.'

Lindsey headed down the hallway. Coming toward him, captain's bars shining on her uniform collar, was Dorothy Yamura. Her hair was no longer the glossy sable it had been when last Lindsey had seen her. Now it was streaked with gray. But otherwise she appeared unchanged. Lindsey wondered if she would recognize him. He did not wonder long.

'Mr. Lindsey! I heard you were in the building. Is this a social call?'

Had Strombeck alerted Yamura that Lindsey was poking around in police matters again? Or was their encounter a coincidence? Dorothy Yamura did not give any indication of which was the case.

'I thought I was retired,' Lindsey told her, 'but here I am back in harness after all this time.'

'I hope Sergeant Strombeck was helpful.'

'It's a start.' Lindsey paused, then asked, 'Is Sergeant Plum still on the force?'

Again a pause, but this time there was more information coming. More, but not much more. 'Yes.'

'I'd love to say hello.' *You bet I would!*

'I'm afraid she's out of the building just now.'

'When will she be back? Tomorrow morning?'

Yamura frowned. 'Tell you what, Mr. Lindsey. I'll get a message to her. Are you staying in Berkeley?'

'Emeryville. I'll be at the Woodfin for a while.'

Yamura looked impressed. 'Nice surroundings. I trust you're on an expense account.' She smiled.

Lindsey found another International Surety card, scribbled Woodfin on the back and handed it to Yamura.

She escorted him to the lobby. He turned in his visitor's badge and stepped out of the building, into brilliant late-afternoon sunlight. He'd come into Berkeley on public transit and rented a car on International Surety's dime. The Avenger was safely garaged in a Center Street facility.

Feeling stale, Lindsey headed toward Berkeley's modest downtown on foot. There were the usual changes, businesses coming and going, pedestrians' fashions evolving along with the rest of the world. Business-suited professionals mingled with jeans-wearing high school and college students and ragged street people.

Berkeley had lost much of its fabled radicalism, but it was still a progressive town whose character was dominated by a huge university. Further from police headquarters Lindsey came to fabled Telegraph Avenue. That street had changed little in the years since he'd first tackled a case there. A seemingly worthless cache of comic books had been burgled from a specialty shop, and when the owner filed a claim the local International Surety branch manager had turned pale, then bright red, then sent Hobart Lindsey to look into the matter.

The routine insurance matter had turned into a murder investigation, and Lindsey had found himself working with then Officer Marvia Plum, the first African American with whom he had had more than a passing acquaintance. That case had changed Lindsey's career, making him a rising star at International Surety. And Marvia Plum had changed his life.

The biggest change on Telegraph Avenue was the disappearance of a landmark bookstore. Lindsey stood gazing at the vacant building. He asked a scholarly-looking individual what had happened and was rewarded with a wry smile. 'General Motors got a bailout, Citibank got a bailout, Cody's Books went belly up. Sometimes mismanagement pays, sometimes it doesn't.'

Lindsey found a quiet restaurant near the campus. It was in an old building and had the atmosphere of a monastery's refectory. He had a good meal, treated himself to a glass of red wine, and strolled back to the garage for the Avenger. Minutes later he was settled in his hotel room. He had a soothing view of San Francisco Bay, a big-screen TV, and an internet connection.

He had nearly finished writing up his notes for the day, preparatory to sending them to SPUDS headquarters in Denver, when he heard the knock. He put his laptop to sleep and crossed the room to open the door.

For a moment it seemed that time stood still; neither of them said a word or moved a muscle. Then they moved simultaneously, he toward her, she toward him. Then they were in his hotel room, the door closed behind them, their arms around each other. To Lindsey's astonishment he found himself crying.

Then they dropped their arms as if embarrassed. Was it embarrassment, Lindsey wondered, or something else? What else? He had no idea. He was not an emotional man. Since his enforced early retirement from International Surety, he had lived quietly in the house where he had grown up. His mother had remarried. The former Mrs. Joe Lindsey, widow, was now Mrs. Gordon Sloane. She lived with her husband in a senior community in the town of Carlsbad, California, near San Diego. Lindsey had spent his time reading, watching old motion pictures, filling his mental Rolodex with trivia about the entertainment world of Mother's era, tending a modest garden, and waiting for middle age to turn into old age so he could move into a senior community near San Diego.

Instead . . . instead — he was breathless.

The two of them crossed the room hand in hand, like children taking courage from each other in the darkness, except that this room was by no means dark. They sat on a characterless hotel-room sofa holding hands.

Lindsey studied Marvia Plum. Her hair was cropped short. Her face — she might have gained a few pounds, but her face was hardly changed. She wore civilian clothes. Nothing to draw the eye, nothing to attract attention to the outfit or the person. A lightweight jacket, a plaid shirt with a button-up front and a button-down collar, moderately faded jeans, flat shoes. In a town like Berkeley you passed a hundred Marvia Plums in an afternoon and didn't really notice one of them. The only place where she'd stand out would be a town where anybody with black skin was noticed.

When they spoke they spoke simultaneously.

'Dorothy Yamura told me you were looking for me.'

'Dorothy Yamura told me you were still on the force.'

'It's funny.'

'It's funny.'

Finally, she put her hand on his mouth, to stop him from speaking, to caress her one-time lover. He leaned forward and pressed his cheek to her head. He wasn't as tall as he might have been, but he was tall enough to do this. After a moment he straightened.

'Hobart, it's been a long time since we worked together.'

'That arms collector in Marin.'

She dropped her hand back to her lap. 'What's this about the Simmons homicide?'

'It's an insurance matter,' he said.

'Same as always.'

'What about — ' He started to say 'us' but his courage failed and instead he said, ' — you? What about you and your family? Your mother? Tyrone and Jamie?'

'My mother's gone. Died two years ago. I warned her to calm down. She was a perfect candidate for a stroke and she had one. At least she went fast; that was a mercy. She could never have coped with being disabled.'

'I'm sorry.'

She nodded. 'We never got along, you know. I think she was frustrated. I think she had dreams as a girl; wanted to . . . I don't really know, Hobart. I'm not sure that she knew herself. But those were the old days. There wasn't much chance for a black woman. She got out of the ghetto and made a decent living. She had a good husband. But forty years of shuffling papers in a rabbit warren — she wanted more. I think so, anyway. And she laid her hopes on me.' She paused, then: 'Do you have anything to drink, Bart?'

'You mean alcohol?'

She nodded.

'I'll call room service.'

'No. Let's go out instead.'

'Yes, let's.'

In the elevator, Lindsey said, 'I don't really know this town. Not anymore. Where should we go?'

'What's your pick, noisy or quiet?'

'Noisy.'

She drove a battered Ford Falcon. As Lindsey climbed in he said, 'Your brother still in the mechanic business?'

'He's got a shop on San Pablo. Takes customers only by referral, and there's a waiting list.'

Marvia tapped a button on the dashboard and the car was filled with the sound of a Bach harpsichord piece. She guided the Falcon under the freeway and parked at a converted railroad station. The sign over the entrance said 'Brennan's — Since 1959.' The bartender, a woman with short-cropped hair and a welcoming smile, greeted Marvia. Marvia introduced

Lindsey and the bartender shook his hand. She had a warm, firm grip.

The bartender poured a straight shot for Marvia and sent an inquiring look at Lindsey. He said, 'I'll have the same.'

Marvia grinned at him. 'Well, you've decided to drink like a man.'

He lifted his glass. They clicked them together and each tossed back a shot.

When the bartender refilled their glasses, Lindsey held his at eye level. Observed through the amber fluid, the scene at the bar looked like a moment in a film noir, an odd sepia print. In his mind's eye the drinkers were transformed into William Bendix, Lizabeth Scott, Robert Mitchum, and Jane Greer. The bartender was Mercedes McCambridge.

He lowered the glass and shook his head to clear it of the image. 'I'm glad Tyrone's all right,' he said. 'I remember that old Volvo he upgraded for me. Sometimes I wish I still had it, but I decided to sell it when I.S. sent me to Europe.'

Marvia's eyes widened. 'Europe?'

'Had to go to Italy. Nasty case. One of

my colleagues was murdered.'

'In Italy?'

'Sorry, no. In New York. Of course, the police in New York weren't happy to have this insurance man from Colorado — I was working out of Denver — poking around their case. But there was some hanky-panky with corporate funds, and I wound up having to work on that angle. Wound up in Rome. That didn't last long, but corporate got wind of it and I wound up back there for a few years. *Capeesh Italiano?*'

She laughed and shook her head.

'Me neither. Not really. I picked up enough to take a taxi or order a meal. After a while I could even buy a pair of *scarpe*.'

Marvia gave him a puzzled look.

'Shoes. I've forgotten most of it by now. Use it or lose it.' They were silent, surrounded by voices and activity. There were half a dozen TVs playing. Lindsey said, 'What about your son?'

'Jamie's made it. My mother would be happy, I think. He works at Pixar. Studied computer animation. He lived cartoons when he was a kid. Remember Jamie and his friend Hakeem White?'

Lindsey said he did.

'I had a time keeping those kids out of trouble. Jamie smoked dope and stole a few things. Always pushing the envelope. Hakeem's family was so strict, he couldn't go to school without polishing his shoes and putting a knot in his tie.'

'I remember.'

'They both made it, Hobart. For once in my life I think I did something right. Jamie's a manager at Pixar now.' Marvia paused.

'What about his pal Hakeem White?' Lindsey prompted.

Marvia's expression was uncertain. 'He got a great job doing software development up in Seattle. I think he was just as happy to get away from that strict religious home life as he was to get his career going. Then his dad died. His mom had been fading, but his dad seemed to be as strong as ever, then — a fatal heart attack. No warning. Left the house to go to work and fell over.'

'What about his wife, then? If she was in failing health, what then?'

'Hakeem resigned from his job and moved back to care for his mom. I hardly ever see him, just leaving the house for work and coming back at night.' Another pause, then Marvia brightened. 'I guess I did all right with Jamie. When his father dumped me, the only thing I got out of him was a last name for my son. At least there was that. There was a time . . . ' She downed her second drink, put her hand on Lindsey's and said, 'What about this case, Bart? What are you doing in Berkeley?'

'Same old thing. Nothing dramatic. Marvia, is this official? Are you on duty?'

'You mean the old never-drink-on-duty thing? That's half a myth, you know. Undercover, developing a suspect, late at night in a sleazy bar, and you tell the bartender, 'I'll have a right fresh glass of that there sarsaparilla, ma'am.' I don't think so. But it just so happens that I'm officially off duty anyway.'

'Is that why you're in civvies? I got a weird response from Strombeck when I asked about you. And from Dorothy Yamura, too.'

'Gordon Simmons was my friend's husband. I have a little account at that savings and loan where Angela works. We were acquaintances, then friends. When her husband was killed, it broke her up.'

'I talked with her. She seems to be doing all right.'

'It's been a year. BPD has a lot of other things on its plate, but I'm still working the Simmons case. Can we leave it at that?'

Lindsey shook his head. 'I don't think so. I'm working on it, too.'

'In a different way, Hobart. What are you really after?'

He felt sheepish. What was a copyright suit compared to a murder case? Still . . . He explained it to Marvia. He concluded, 'I think the answer is on Gordon Simmons's laptop.'

'I think we'll crack this case from both angles if we find that computer,' Marvia agreed.

She offered him a ride back to his hotel in her battered Falcon. It didn't run like an unrestored relic. When Lindsey commented on it Marvia said, 'Protective coloration, Hobart. Tyrone's magic. This is a Falcon on the outside but it's a V-eight Mustang on the inside.'

At the Woodfin they exchanged cell-phone numbers. 'Strictly unofficial, Hobart. Anything official goes through Olaf Strombeck. He's a good man. But keep me posted. I'll do the same for you.'

Later, in his hotel room, Lindsey turned on a late-night movie. He missed the opening credits but he recognized it anyway; he'd seen it half a dozen times. Rosalind Russell as Valerie Stanton, a Broadway comedian with an itch to play Ibsen. Sydney Greenstreet as a middle-aged homicide detective — massive, immobile, self-mocking, ironic, polite. And patient. Prodding, prodding. Ultimately invincible.

Somebody had been reading Rex Stout. Why Greenstreet's character was Captain Danbury instead of Nero Wolfe was a greater mystery than who killed Gordon Dunning. Probably a copyright problem.

4

Gordian House wasn't a house at all. Not that Lindsey expected it to be one, but he'd looked forward to something more impressive than a dingy office suite on the sixth floor of an aging commercial building on Shattuck Avenue. The furnishings looked as if they hadn't been changed since Ike was president.

There was actually a Remington Standard on the receptionist's desk and a half-height wooden room divider with a swinging door in it. The only thing missing was a PBX switchboard. They probably kept that in the storage closet, waiting for time to flow backward.

The receptionist looked as if she couldn't decide whether she was an unreconstructed hippie chick or a frowsy housewife, but when Lindsey presented his card she buzzed him through to an inner office. That was no more modern and no less dingy than the outer chamber.

There was only one desk in the room, with a small sign reading 'Jack Burnside.'

The shirtsleeved man behind the desk looked to be in his sixties, with unkempt graying hair and a bushy mustache to match. He stood up, removed a half-smoked cigar from his mouth, and snarled, 'I hope you're not from the goddamned tobacco police.'

Lindsey said, 'No, no. Nothing like that.'

Was Burnside joking, or was there really such a thing as the tobacco police in this town? Never mind. Lindsey presented his card. 'I'm from International Surety. We carry your liability policy.'

'I know that, I know that.' Burnside transferred the cigar to his other hand and extended a callused paw to Lindsey, then gestured him to a battered wooden chair. 'Look, I don't know what these high-tone bluebloods at Marston and Morse have against an honest businessman. Christ, Linsley — '

'Lindsey.'

'That's what I said. Look, I've been in this racket all my life. You know I worked with Aaron Wyn in New York? I sold pictures for Irving Klaw. You wouldn't believe it, but I once put a move on Bettie Page. So innocent she didn't even know what was going on. But there was some hot, hot stuff. I mean, hot. I worked for Hamling in Chicago. I gave Milton Luros his start. I was publishing pulps that would make a Donnenfeld blush, and Miltie painted covers for me.' He leaned back in his chair. 'These snooty SOBs want to put me out of business. I'll fight the bastards. I'll fight 'em all the way. I'll whip their asses in court.'

Lindsey raised his hand. Burnside grunted acknowledgement but he kept on rolling. 'There's no way they can beat me, but if they do it's on your backside, not mine. International Sure-As-Hell, that's what I call you guys. International Sure-As-Hell. If I lose — no way I lose; I'm going to clank their clock, those arrogant SOBs — but if they do win, International Sure-As-Hell has to pay, not Gordian House.' He paused again to draw on his cigar.

Before he could resume, Lindsey said, 'Mr. Burnside — '

'Jack. Call me Jack. What's your first name?' He squinted at Lindsey's business card. 'Hobart. Hobart. What the hell kind of name is that? I think I bought a Hobart stove one time. Or was it a dishwasher? My wife buys these things. I give her an allowance. I don't know what she does with the money half the time.'

'Yes, well, that's my name. You'd have to ask my mother how she picked it. All right, Jack — what I need to know is your side of this story.'

'You been talking to those snobs at Murder and Monkeyshines?'

'No, sir, I haven't talked to them yet. I hope I can get this matter straightened out. If Gordian House is blameless, I hope we can convince the other side to drop their case. If not, International Surety will try and work out a settlement. We don't want a court fight and I hope they don't want one either. Nobody wins that kind of battle except for the lawyers.'

'You want to hear my side?'

Lindsey nodded.

'I already told my lawyer all about it. What's-her-name Caswell. J. P. Caswell.

Won't even use a first name. I call her Jaypee. Firm is Hopkins, MacKinney, Black. In Oakland.'

'Yes, I'll talk with them. With Ms. Caswell. But I'd like to hear it in your own words.'

'Okay. Here we go.'

He pushed himself up and opened a door to another room. Lindsey peered through the doorway. The room was full of modern equipment. A crew of young men and women sat at computers, busily clicking away at their keyboards. Burnside disappeared. Lindsey waited. Burnside reappeared, closed the door behind him, and tossed a paperback book at Lindsey. Lindsey managed to catch it. He turned it over and studied the package.

The cover painting showed a woman wearing an off-the-shoulder blouse and a short, tight skirt sitting on a barstool. A tough-looking unshaven male in a T-shirt and jeans had one hand on her thigh. His other hand held a revolver. The whole scene was framed in a porthole-shaped window. The title of the book, lettered in simulated neon tubing, was *The Emerald Cat*.

'This is the *casus belli*?' Lindsey asked.

'The what?'

'The cause of all the trouble.'

'Yeah, right. See the byline on that thing?'

Lindsey read it aloud. 'Steve Damon.' He opened the book and looked at the copyright page. The book was credited to Gordian House, Inc. 'Why isn't it copyrighted by the author?'

Burnside said, 'Huh. We bought it. Agent sold it to us. What they call work done for hire, even though it wasn't done for us. But it's ours now.'

'You bought it from Steve Damon?'

'Nope. His agent.'

'All right, then I'll need to talk to Mr. Damon's agent.'

Burnside opened a desk drawer and pulled out a Rolodex. 'Here you go.' He flipped cards until he found the one he wanted. 'Rachael Gottlieb.' He read off a Berkeley address. 'Says she's Damon's agent. She signed the contract, he signed it, too. Signed, sealed, and delivered. Check went to Gottlieb. I guess she took her pound of flesh and gave the rest to

Damon, but I wouldn't know for certain. Maybe she screwed him out of it. No pun intended, Linsley. No skin off my back either way.'

Lindsey jotted Gottlieb's name and address in his organizer and slipped it back into his pocket. 'So you never actually met Damon.'

'Nope. Never talk to authors. I have people to do that.' He gestured toward the door that led to the high-tech room. 'Don't think anybody talked to him, though. I handled this one myself. Met Gottlieb. Nice piece. Tight jeans, what the kids wear nowadays. Made me wish I was twenty years younger.'

Forty would be more like it, Lindsey thought. He stood up. 'All right. Thank you, ah, Jack. I'll be in touch. Thanks for the book.'

'Any time. Any time. Say hello to my girl on the way out.'

Lindsey said hello to Burnside's receptionist on the way out.

Shortly, in the building lobby, he studied the address Burnside had given him for Rachael Gottlieb. Dana Street.

He remembered that from past years.

He was about to retrieve his rented Avenger from the parking garage and head for the Gottlieb Literary Agency, but standing in the bright sunlight of Shattuck Avenue he realized that he wasn't ready to meet Damon's agent. Not quite yet. Instead, he walked the short distance to the Berkeley Public Library, settled himself in the airy, high-ceilinged reading room, and opened the copy of *The Emerald Cat* that Jack Burnside had tossed at him. It was a short novel, less than two hundred pages, and Lindsey felt no need to study every paragraph of Steve Damon's deathless prose. He could get a reasonable take on the book by skimming, and in fact an hour's attention proved sufficient.

The Emerald Cat seemed to be a standard hardboiled murder mystery. The title referred to a sleazy bar on San Pablo Avenue in El Cerrito, a town just north of Berkeley. It had obviously been written in the recent past, as the author wrote at length about the Emerald Cat's Dutch doors. Smokers could stand inside the tavern while leaning over the half-door and getting their nicotine fix outside the establishment.

Damon's tough-as-nails private eye was one Troy Percheron. Percheron had an equally tough girlfriend. Damon referred to her as a frail, bringing a grin to Lindsey's face. Her name was Helena Cairo. She was obviously the sexy woman featured on the cover of the book.

There was a fairly brutal murder, its motive not quite clear to Lindsey. The victim was one Henry Blank. It wasn't altogether clear to Lindsey why Blank had been garroted, either; but after a series of chases, beatings, drunken interludes, sexual encounters described in almost as much detail as Percheron's battles with fists, brass knuckles, and tire chains, Percheron subdued the killer, a gigantic brute known as Frank 'Frankenstein' Farmer, and turned him over to the local gendarmerie.

Lindsey wasn't exactly an authority on hardboiled dick novels. He knew the genre more from films *noir*, but he'd read a couple of Chandlers and a sampling of

Spillanes, enough to know what they were like. As far as he could tell, Steve Damon was an average practitioner of the craft.

He breathed a sigh of relief, slipped the paperback into his jacket pocket, and headed for the garage. Traffic wasn't too heavy and he reached his destination in a matter of minutes.

He'd expected the Gottlieb Literary Agency to be located in an office building like the one that housed Gordian House, but in fact he found himself standing in front of a well-maintained Victorian. He looked at the address in his organizer again, then at the house number. He climbed the steps and found a row of doorbells.

There was a handwritten card marked simply 'Gottlieb' next to the buzzer for 4A. Maybe this was the agent's home. Why would Burnside give him her home address rather than that of her office?

He rang the bell and was answered with a loud buzzing, then pressed the latch and the door opened. He made his way to apartment 4A. A young woman greeted him at the door.

Jack Burnside's vulgar description of Rachael Gottlieb might have been fairly accurate for a twenty-something female with an olive complexion, reasonably attractive features, and dark hair drawn back in a ponytail. She was attired in blue jeans and a sweatshirt with a picture of a woman Lindsey did not recognize on the chest.

She looked questioningly at Lindsey. He introduced himself, proffered his business card, and said, 'Miss Gottlieb?'

She admitted as much. From the apartment behind her Lindsey could hear voices raised in slow rhythm. The effect was not unpleasant. There were rugs and cushions on the floor and a narrow column of gray rising from a hammered brass incense burner.

The young woman inquired the nature of Lindsey's business. He asked if she was indeed Steve Damon's literary agent, Rachael Gottlieb. She was. He wondered if this was a convenient time to discuss a business matter involving Mr. Damon. Or would she prefer to meet him at her office?

'This *is* my office.' She had a soft voice that would have been at home with the singing — more like chanting — from inside the apartment. 'You can come in.'

Either Rachael Gottlieb couldn't afford much furniture, or she preferred to do without it. Lindsey found himself seated on a floor cushion, listening to recorded sounds.

Rachael Gottlieb left the room briefly, returned carrying a cast-iron pot, and poured a cup for Lindsey. 'It's *pu-erh*. It's very soothing. I find that it harmonizes the body with the music of Hildegard. A most astonishing woman, Hildegard von Bingen. Do you know the 'Antiphon for Saint Ursula'? It elevates the spirit.' She lowered the cast-iron pot to a three-legged trivet and herself to a floor cushion, facing Lindsey. 'Now, Mr. Lindsey, what do you wish to know?'

Lindsey sipped the *pu-erh* tea. He didn't know whether it would harmonize his body or not, but it tasted good. He said that he was investigating an alleged plagiarism case involving Steve Damon and asked if Miss Gottlieb could put him in touch with the author.

'That's not so easy.'

Lindsey asked why not.

'I'm afraid he's dropped the class.'

Lindsey frowned. 'I'm sorry, you're losing me. What class is that? Aren't you an agent? Isn't he your client?'

'We were taking a class together at Laney. You know Laney College, in Oakland?'

'I know of it.'

' "Female Poets from Sumangalamata to Maya Angelou." You see?' She waved a hand gracefully toward a small stack of books. Lindsey didn't recognize many of the bylines but he was willing to take her word.

'Rigoberto was the only man in the class. He — ' She stopped when she saw Lindsey's frown.

'Rigoberto?'

'Oh. Steve Damon is a pseudonym. Rigoberto, Rigoberto Chocron, was in the class. We went out for coffee afterwards — it was an evening class — we went out for coffee a few times and he told me he'd written a novel and he didn't know how to market it. I told him he should ask Professor Rostum, Rosemary Rostum — she taught our poetry class. But he thought she wouldn't like his book. So I suggested that he just go to the library and get a directory of publishers and try to sell it himself. But he didn't want to.' She paused to sip her own *pu-erh*.

Lindsey asked if Damon Chocron had said why he didn't want to market the book himself.

'He'd been in a certain amount of trouble. He was getting a stipend from some kind of rehabilitation people for going to school. He seemed afraid of publicity; asked if I'd do it for him. I thought maybe he was just shy. Anyway, I looked up local publishers and there was Gordian House, so I called them up and went to see Mr. Burnside, and he bought the book. That's about all there was to it. I didn't even take a commission. I just cashed the Gordian House check and paid Rigoberto in cash. He said he didn't have a bank account and he couldn't cash a check himself.'

Lindsey asked Rachael Gottlieb for Chocron's address.

'I don't have it. He dropped out of the class. I think he dropped out of Laney altogether. He was a pretty elusive character, as a matter of fact.' She paused and tilted her head to one side — listening, Lindsey decided, to the gentle voices, women's voices, coming from a set of speakers in the corners of the room. She smiled. 'He told me he has a favorite restaurant where he picks up telephone messages. I can give you that.'

Lindsey took it with thanks. He got to his feet, not as quickly or easily as he might have a few decades earlier. He thanked Rachael Gottlieb for her help.

Just at the doorway he stopped and turned back, feeling like Peter Falk in a rumpled trench coat. 'Just one more thing, Miss Gottlieb.'

She nodded, holding her cup of *pu-erh* tea to her lips, smiling amusedly at him over the rim. Lindsey decided that she was a *Columbo* fan after all.

'How did Mr. Damon — Chocron — give you his book?'

She looked puzzled.

'I mean, was it a typewritten manuscript, or a computer printout, or — you see?'

'Oh, yes. It was on a disk. Mr. Burnside said they don't bother with paper manuscripts anymore. They ask their authors to email their manuscripts, or else to turn them in on CDs. I told Rigoberto and he said okay, he'd download the book and give me the CD at our next class. That was before he dropped out.'

'Do you know anything about his computer?'

She smiled gently. 'No. No, I don't. Good-bye, Mr. Lindsey. I hope you enjoyed the *pu-erh* tea.' She floated to her feet and crossed the room to close the door.

On the porch of the Dana Street house, Lindsey blinked at the late afternoon sunlight, wondering how long he had spent in Rachael Gottlieb's apartment listening to Hildegard's music. Whoever Hildegard was. He checked his watch. Next stop — ? He had to make a plan.

He returned to his hotel room, opened his own laptop, plugged it into a phone jack, and sent a report to Denver. Then he did a web search for Marston and Morse, Publishers, and placed a phone call. He made an appointment for the following morning.

He closed down the laptop and stretched out on the hotel bed. It wasn't time for dinner yet. He'd earned his day's pay from International Surety. He kicked off his shoes and burrowed into the pillow to take a nap. Somehow the nap stretched into a good night's sleep. He must have awakened enough to climb out of his clothes during the night, because he woke up with sunlight streaming through the window and his clothing neatly hung in the closet.

5

Marston and Morse, Publishers, was located in a new building on University Avenue. The company occupied a suite on the top floor. The decor was a combination of modern efficiency and green chic. There were plants in the lobby and a female receptionist who had to be older than she looked.

Lindsey extended his International Surety card. She took it, then whispered into a bead-mike mounted on a hair-thin wire, smiled at Lindsey and said, 'Please have a seat. Mrs. Morse will be right with you.'

Very soon Lindsey found himself facing a slim business-suited woman in her fifties. At least, her silver-gray hair said as much. Her unlined face could have said thirty. Her deep green eyes could have said anything.

'Mr. Lindsey, won't you please come in?' She led the way into a comfortable office. Large windows faced the bay. They were high enough in the building that Lindsey could see Alcatraz Island, the Golden Gate Bridge and the Marin Highlands.

'I'm Paula Paige Morse. I'm the president and editor-in-chief of Marston and Morse. I understand that you're investigating this *Emerald Cat* matter. What can I do to be helpful?'

Lindsey said, 'I want to be honest with you, Mrs. Morse. My company insures Gordian House. If your claim against them holds up, International Surety stands to lose a good deal of money.'

'Of course.' She was seated opposite Lindsey. They were in matching chairs, separated only by a blond-wood coffee table. The walls, between well-stocked bookcases, featured some very good abstract paintings. And they didn't look like prints. 'I hope that doesn't create ill will between us. Marston and Morse doesn't operate that way. We prefer to think of Gordian House and ourselves as fellow problem-solvers.'

She's actually serious, Lindsey thought.

In this day and age. Truly amazing. He said, 'I'd like to hear Marston and Morse's side of this complaint.'

'Marston and Morse isn't a very large company, but it's been in business since the 1950s. Delbert Marston was a popular novelist who wrote for Paige Publications in Chicago. They published mainly paperback fiction. A lot of it was fairly lurid. And, yes, in case you were wondering, Delbert Marston was my great-uncle. Mr. Marston had his eye on more literary productions. In the 1960s, he moved to the west coast and started a company of his own, publishing literary biographies, philosophy, poetry, and what we like to think of as serious, quality fiction.'

She stood up and walked to the side of the room. 'He had a partner, Paul Morse. In time, Paul Morse had a son, Paul Junior. Delbert Marston stayed in touch with Paige Publications, and eventually — well, stranger things have happened. I wound up married to Paul Junior. Both Paul Senior and Delbert Marston are deceased now, but we kept the name.'

'But this *Emerald Cat* situation — '

'Yes, I'm sorry. Marston and Morse finally absorbed Paige Publications. We've kept a few of their old titles in print. It's a sentimental gesture, I suppose. Only a small part of our business. And we do issue an occasional pulp paperback. It's a guilty pleasure of the publishing business, I suppose.'

She removed a handful of paperbacks from a bookshelf and spread them on the table between herself and Lindsey. 'Oh,' she said, 'how discourteous of me! Would you like a cup of tea, Mr. Lindsey? Or coffee?'

Lindsey declined the offer. The books looked oddly familiar. 'This may surprise you, Mrs. Morse, but I was once involved in a life insurance settlement in Chicago, and I met a Patricia Paige.'

'My aunt Patti!'

'As I recall, she didn't like her name. People kept confusing her with a popular vocalist of the 1950s.'

'Oh, I know, I know.'

Suddenly Paula Paige Morse looked like a college girl. 'I remember how much she hated that song, 'How Much is that Doggie in the Window?'' She had a lovely laugh.

Lindsey scanned the old paperbacks. *Buccaneer Blades*, by Violet de la Yema. *Cry Ruffian!* by Salvatore Pescara. *Teen Gangs of Chicago* by Anonymous. *Death in the Ditch* by Del Marston.

'And lately we've published a series of detective novels by a local author, Gordon Simmons. He wrote as Wallace Thompson. Quite good books, of their sort. He wrote about a private detective called Tony Clydesdale and his girlfriend, Selena Thebes. I can give you copies of the books if you'd like. We'd published eight of them and Gordon was working on the ninth. He'd been in the office and told us that he'd finished a draft and just had to polish it up before turning it in — when he died.'

'Was murdered.'

'Yes.'

'We never got that book. Angela Simmons, Gordon's wife, told us that the book existed only as a computer file. You know how they keep saying, *back up your work, back up your work*, but Gordon didn't remember to back up that last book. When his killer made off with Gordon's laptop computer, he took the only copy of the book with him. *The Ruby Red Pup*, that was the name of the book. There's a sleazy bar on San Pablo Avenue in El Cerrito with that name.'

Paula Paige Morse slipped back into her chair and drew a deep breath. 'This is where the story gets ugly. Uglier, I should say.' She said it sadly. 'Apparently Tony Clydesdale had a following of loyal readers. One of them called the office. I spoke with him myself. He sounded very upset.'

Lindsey asked the fan's name. Apparently Paula Paige Morse had a memory for names. 'Jemmy Ruhlman. Jemmy, short for Jeremy. He's a student at UC. Said that he and friends had read all the Tony Clydesdale novels and had trivia contests about them.'

She gathered up the old Paige Publications paperbacks and restored them to their place on the bookshelf. 'Jemmy was very upset. He'd been in a little bookstore up on Claremont Avenue, an odd place called Dark Carnival, browsing through their mystery section, and he came across a book called *The Emerald Cat*. The cover caught his eye, he told me, and he wound up reading the book. He said it was a Tony Clydesdale novel in every way — the setting, the narrative structure, the author's style. And Jemmy said this was absolutely a Wallace Thompson book.'

She drew a deep breath. She was the picture of *I'm-sorry-to-tell-you-this-but . . .* 'Only instead of the Ruby Red Pup on San Pablo, the setting was a sleazy bar on Solano Avenue called the Emerald Cat. Tony Clydesdale had become Troy Percheron. Selena Thebes had become Helena Cairo. You see, the author of *The Emerald Cat* must not have had much imagination. Either that or he was awfully lazy. Turning Tony Clydesdale into Troy Percheron, Selena Thebes into Helena Cairo . . . well, really.'

'And you think this Steve Damon, the author of *The Emerald Cat*, killed Simmons? Mrs. Morse, that's a matter for the police, don't you see?'

'Of course. I've spoken with a Sergeant

Strombeck about it. The trouble is, nobody can find Steve Damon. It's probably a pseudonym. Steve Damon could be anybody. But under the name Steve Damon — why, apparently there's no such person.'

Lindsey rubbed his eyes. He knew that. At least, according to Rachael Gottlieb, Steve Damon was Rigoberto Chocron. If there was such a person as Rigoberto Chocron. Masks behind masks, deception behind deception.

And if Olaf Strombeck had got this far with the case — had followed the trail, possibly from Angela Simmons to Paula Paige Morse — he would almost certainly know about Steve Damon. Would he have traced Damon back to Rachael Gottlieb? If so, he would surely have learned that Damon was really Chocron. Why hadn't he mentioned that to Lindsey? Maybe the straight-as-a-string perfect cop had something to hide, too.

'We've tried to work things out with Gordian House,' Paula Paige Morse was saying. 'But I'm afraid Mr. Burnside is not an easy man to deal with.'

Focus, Lindsey! Focus! He needed to

bring the conversation back to the issue at hand. He was an insurance investigator, not a homicide detective. International Surety's client was Gordian House. His job was to determine whether it made more sense for Gordian to settle with Marston and Morse or to fight them in court. Finding Gordon Simmons's killer was the police department's job, not his.

He thanked Paula Paige Morse for her hospitality. She told him that she hoped the dispute could be settled without going to court. He agreed. She saw him to the door, asked her receptionist to get him a selection of Tony Clydesdale mysteries, and turned back toward her own office.

Lindsey stood on the sidewalk, watching traffic whiz by on University Avenue. Then he found a café, ordered a cappuccino and a croissant, opened his pocket organizer and turned on his cell phone. He punched in the number Rachael Gottlieb had given him for Rigoberto Chocron's favorite restaurant.

The person who answered apparently spoke only Spanish. Lindsey had a few words of that language and hoped that he got his message across. He left his cell-phone number and nursed his cappuccino.

He used the time to skim a couple of the books he'd received from Paula Paige Morse's receptionist. *The Orange Owl. The Turquoise Tortoise.* The covers were less lurid than the one on Gordian House's *The Emerald Cat*, and the production quality was substantially better. He read the opening scene of *The Orange Owl*, then skipped ahead a few chapters, sampled a few pages, skipped and sampled, switched to *The Turquoise Turtle* and repeated.

There was no question in his mind: Troy Percheron and Helena Cairo were copied from Tony Clydesdale and Selena Thebes. No, they weren't just copies. They *were* the characters from Gordon Simmons's — 'Wallace Thompson's' — hardboiled novels. This was not good news for Gordian House and it was not good news for International Surety, but it was the truth.

After a while he punched in the number Marvia Plum had given him for her own cell phone. The phone rang a few times and then he was switched to voice-mail. For a moment he considered calling Strombeck at BPD, but instead left a brief message for Marvia and went back to waiting.

The phone rang. A heavily accented voice said, 'Mr. Lindsey?'

'Is this Rigoberto Chocron?'

'Rachael says you want to talk to me.'

'Yes, please.'

'Why?' Rigoberto Chocron didn't mince words.

'It's about your book,' Lindsey said. 'It's about *The Emerald Cat*.'

'What about it?'

'It's an insurance matter, Mr. Chocron.'

There was a pause. Lindsey could hear the clatter of silverware and dishes in the background. Then Chocron said, 'Look, what's in it for me?'

'That depends on what you can give me,' Lindsey said.

'I didn't do nothing wrong,' Chocron said. 'I just wrote a book. Why you coming after me?'

'Just for some information. There's a dispute between two publishing houses.

One of them has an insurance policy with my company and I need to file a report.'

'Yeah, sure. I believe you.'

Fat chance of that!

Chocron said, 'You want to talk to me, you gotta pay for my time.'

'And how much would that be worth?'

'I don't know. How does five hundred an hour sound?'

Lindsey thought fast. It was International Surety's money, not his. He might get a bonus if he cracked this case, saving I.S. a fat settlement with Marston and Morse. But if Chocron had killed Gordon Simmons, he was a dangerous man. Damn it, why didn't Marvia Plum return his call? Again, he considered calling Olaf Strombeck. Maybe . . .

'Come on, man.' Rigoberto Chocron was getting impatient. 'I can't hang around all day.'

'I was thinking more of a hundred.'

'A hundred?' Chocron sounded angry. 'Forget about it. You think you can get me cheap like some poor illegal? I was born here. I got rights.'

Lindsey said, 'All right. What about

three? Three hundred. When and where do we meet?'

'Not so fast, *amigo*. Three is better than one but it's still not enough.'

Lindsey said, 'All right. Let's say I guarantee three. If the information is good enough, it can be more than that. Maybe even five.'

There was a long silence. Now Lindsey started doubting himself. Why hadn't he just agreed to five? What if he'd blown off a valuable lead, a source who could provide information worth thousands — might even crack the whole case — to save International Surety a few hundred dollars?

Now Rigoberto Chocron's voice came from the cell phone. 'You come here. Tell you what, you come up with the five, I'll even buy you a good meal.' He gave Lindsey an address in Fruitvale, Oakland's thriving Latino district.

'How will I know you?' Lindsey asked.

'Don't you worry. I'll know you. Don't stand me up. You owe me five.'

The drive from downtown Berkeley to Fruitvale took half an hour. Lindsey found the street Chocron had named, parked his rented Dodge Avenger, and walked toward the number. The street was bustling with pedestrians, school kids, mothers pushing strollers. The dominant language was Spanish. Young men operated open-air sidewalk shops selling what were obviously bootleg DVDs of first-run movies. Walnut Creek was nothing like this. Lindsey felt as if he'd traveled to a foreign country.

He walked into the restaurant and looked around. It was called Los Arcos de Oro and it had a familiar logo. He wondered if McDonald's knew about it. It was clearly a family business. Most of the tables were occupied. There was a steady buzz of conversation. The only words Lindsey understood were the remnants of lessons that he'd learned in high school forty years before.

He found a vacant table, one of the few in the establishment. He sat down, opened his cell phone, laid it on the table, picked up a menu. Of course, it was entirely in Spanish.

A waitress approached, pad in one hand and pencil in the other. '*Está listo?*' Lindsey hesitated.

A young Latino man appeared behind the waitress and whispered a few words in her ear. She nodded and disappeared into the kitchen. The man looked to be in his late twenties, slim, dark-haired, with a thin mustache. A young Gilbert Roland? He wore blue jeans and an Oakland Raiders T-shirt that showed off tanned, muscular arms.

'You're Hobart Lindsey.' It was the same voice he'd heard on his cell phone, the English fluent but accented.

'Mr. Damon? Or is it Chocron?' Lindsey clicked his cell phone shut, hitting one extra button as he did so. If he got a usable picture of Damon-or-Chocron, that might come in handy.

'Take your pick. You're paying. How does the joke go? 'You can call me anything you want, just don't call me late for dinner.''

'Mr. Chocron, then. Did you write *The Emerald Cat*?'

'I did.'

'That seems very strange to me. I've been — '

Chocron cut him off. 'You have the five hundred?'

Lindsey frowned 'We already discussed that. I'll pay you what the information is worth. Don't worry about that. International Surety is a big company. I'll put in a voucher and you'll receive a check. Normally it takes a month but I can attach an expedite order to it and get it in two weeks.'

Chocron threw his head back and emitted a raucous laugh. Conversation stopped at tables around them and customers turned to stare.

'You're joking, aren't you?'

Lindsey shook his head.

'Well, that won't do.'

The waitress approached again. Chocron nodded to her, and shot out a stream of Spanish. Her pencil danced across her order pad and she scurried away.

'I assure you, International Surety is a reliable company. Their check will be good.'

'I don't do banks, you know? I don't have no bank accounts. They keep too many records. I don't like 'em. How about you just hand me cash?'

'I'll — I'll try to work that out.'

'Not good enough.'

Their waitress was back with two platters of steaming breaded fish with onions. She placed one in front of Lindsey, one in front of Chocron. The food was accompanied by icy glasses and bottles of Negra Modelo.

Lindsey bought time by pouring a dark Mexican beer for himself, sipping it appreciatively, watching the slim waitress weave her way gracefully between tables. After stalling as long as he could, he finally yielded on the money issue. He could use an International Surety credit card at a local ATM and take Chocron's payment out in cash. If Ducky Richelieu or any of the bean counters in Denver had a gripe with that, they could take him off active duty and put him back on the retired list. He hadn't asked for this job.

'But I'll need the information first,' he insisted.

Chocron gave Lindsey a look that would have frozen a bowl of hot lava. He tackled his food, then washed it down with dark beer. 'All right, Mr. Lindsey. I just hope you know who you are dealing with. If I give you what you want and you try to burn me, I can promise you that you will be very sorry.'

That was a pretty good line, Lindsey thought. The kind of threat that Frank Farrar, the murder suspect of *The Emerald Cat*, might have leveled at Troy Percheron just before donning a set of brass knuckles and whaling into the dick.

Chocron said, 'Enjoy your meal and we'll take a little walk.' At least he was as good as his word when it came to paying for Lindsey's meal.

They headed down a shaded residential avenue toward Calle Catorce, the street that Oakland's city fathers had renamed International Boulevard and that everyone in the neighborhood blithely continued to call Fourteenth Street. As they walked, Lindsey said, 'I need information, Mr. Chocron. I need to know about *The Emerald Cat*. There is a serious question as to the actual authorship of the book.'

The younger man smiled. They were near a church. A priest came out of the front door as they passed the church and Chocron exchanged greetings with him.

'Padre.'

'Rigo.'

'I wrote that book,' Chocron told Lindsey.

'Surely you are aware of the similarities between Troy Percheron and your other characters, and Tony Clydesdale and the other figures in Wallace Thompson's detective novels. Not to mention the similarity of the titles themselves.'

'You can't copyright a title. I checked on that. And besides, nobody ever wrote a book called *The Emerald Cat* before I did.'

'Of course. I hope you're not going to say that Clydesdale and Percheron, Thebes and Cairo, are just coincidences. Please, Mr. Chocron, we both know better than that.'

'Why doesn't Thompson complain, then?'

'I'm sorry. I thought you knew he was dead.'

Chocron shook his head. 'Sorry to hear that.' He didn't sound sorry.

'Thompson was a pseudonym. The obituary referred to him by his real name.' There had been a copy of the obit in the case file Lindsey received. 'It didn't mention that he was a mystery writer.'

'What's this to me?' Chocron said.

'Mr. Chocron — '

'Call me Rigo.'

'Yes, yes. We have reason to believe — '

'I'll ask you again, are you a cop? If you are, good-bye, and I hope the fish makes you puke.'

'I'm not a cop, Rigo. I'm an insurance man, that's all. Here.' He gave Chocron his business card and a promotional ball-point pen with the SPUDS logo and *International Surety* laser-engraved on the barrel. Chocron studied the card and the pen and slipped them into his jeans pocket. Lindsey tried again. 'We have reason to believe that the man who used the name Wallace Thompson wrote *The Emerald Cat*. Either that, or essentially that book. When he died — ' No need to go into the details of Gordon Simmons's death. ' — his computer disappeared. A laptop. Mrs. Thompson says that her husband had been working at the library — he had his computer with him and was using it there, and after his death it was never recovered.'

Chocron laughed. 'That thing wasn't worth five hundred dollars. Old and worn out and — '

'You know that?'

Chocron's face fell. 'Son of a gun. Got me, didn't you. All right, what do you really want? You gonna try and get my advance back for Gordian?'

Lindsey shook his head. 'Nothing like that. But if I could get my hands on that computer, I might be able to solve this case.'

They turned a corner onto Calle Catorce. More color, more bustle, more sidewalk vendors, more Spanish in the air.

Chocron frowned, suddenly nervous. 'You wearin' a wire?'

'No, no. Look.' Lindsey peeled back his jacket. 'Nothing. I told you, Rigo, I'm not a police officer, and as far as I know you're not in any trouble. Gordian might try to get their advance back from you, but I don't think they'd have much of a chance. Once a publisher pays an author, they pretty much write off the money.'

'Yeah. And I was so dumb I didn't even

get a royalty deal. There wasn't no advance. Just one check and *adios, amigo*! I guess that was my agent's fault, really, but she's such an innocent spirit I guess she didn't know no better, neither.'

'There's a lawsuit brewing between Gordian House and Thompson's publisher, Marston and Morse. If I can get hold of Thompson's computer I might be able to settle the dispute once and for all. That's all I want from you. The computer itself if you still have it, or a reliable lead to it.'

'I don't have it.'

'Who does?'

'Nobody. I threw it away.'

'I don't believe you.'

'I threw it away,' he repeated angrily.

'Come on, Rigo. You stand to make some nice money. I think you could use it. I need the truth.'

'Five hundred. Cash. Today. You see that bank across Calle Catorce? They got an ATM. I give you what you need, we walk over there and you pull out the money and lay it on me and we never see each other again.'

Lindsey shook his head. 'Not good enough. I told you, Rigo. All right, three hundred guaranteed. The rest depending on what you give me and how good it is.'

'Stop right here.'

They halted in front of a plate-glass window filled with a variety of guitars, mandolins, trumpets, amplifiers, TV sets, clothing, tools, a couple of desktop computers — *and a laptop*. Even a bicycle. Gold lettering on the glass read 'Casa de Empeños.'

Chocron said, 'You know what this place is?'

It couldn't be anything but a pawnshop. Lindsey admitted as much.

'I sold the computer here. Pawned it. I don't know if they still got it. I don't see it in the window.'

Lindsey pointed. 'Isn't that it?'

Chocron shook his head. 'Nope. Look at the logo. Wrong brand. Not mine.' He studied the contents of the window, then said, 'Come on in. I know the *prestamisto*. The pawnbroker.'

6

The *prestamisto* should have been Rod Steiger with a fake mustache and sleeve garters and a green eye-shade, standing behind a barred window and smoking cigarettes furiously. But no such luck.

Lindsey found himself wishing he could plan his strategy with Marvia Plum before talking with the *prestamisto*. Work out a plan with Marvia or with Captain Yamura or Sergeant Strombeck or even, heaven help him, with Ducky Richelieu in Denver. But he couldn't interrupt the proceedings to place a phone call. Rigoberto Chocron was too dicey a character for Lindsey to risk spooking him. Lindsey was relieved that he had turned off his own cell phone.

The *prestamisto* — all right, *prestamista* — was young and eye-catching in a scoop-necked blouse and Mexican skirt. 'Rigo,' she said.

'Crista.'

'What can I do for you today?' She must have pegged Lindsey for a non-Spanish speaker and used English as a courtesy.

Chocron said, 'You remember that laptop I pawned here?'

'I do. You have the ticket with you?'

Chocron dug a battered wallet from his jeans. He fished a printed slip from it and laid it on the counter — a plain, glass-topped counter — in front of the *prestamista*.

Crista picked it up and smiled sadly. 'You know better than this, Rigo. Look at the date.' She laid the slip back on the counter.

Peering over Chocron's shoulder, Lindsey could see the date on the slip.

'You see,' Crista said, 'it's expired. We don't have it anymore. We sold it. But I have some good news for you. We got more than the redemption value. You have some money coming to you. Wait, I'll write you a check.'

Chocron said, 'You know I don't do checks.'

'Oh, that's right.' Apparently the two

were not exactly close, then. 'All right, I can give you cash, but you'll have to sign for it.'

When the transaction was completed, Lindsey asked the *prestamista* if she had a record of the buyer.

Crista smiled. 'I'm sorry, señor, but that's against policy. I cannot tell you that.'

Lindsey felt Rigoberto Chocron's strong fingers on his elbow. 'Just cool it, my friend,' Chocron half-whispered to Lindsey. He moved him bodily away from the counter. Lindsey took the hint and decided to study a fascinating twenty-year-old bright red clock-radio with a major crack running the length of its plastic exterior. There were people who collected such things. If the radio had been intact it might have been worth a couple of hundred dollars to the right buyer. But in its present condition, it would probably be salvaged for parts.

Rigoberto Chocron and the *prestamista* Crista had their heads close together. Chocron was using all his charm on her, stroking her upper arms, whispering in her ear, nodding and gesturing. Cesar

Romero, definitely. All he needed was a *sombrero de diez galónes* with silver trim all over its brim.

Lindsey couldn't hear much of their conversation, and it wouldn't have mattered if he had, for the few words that he caught were in Spanish and he knew that he couldn't have followed the dialogue. Of the words that Lindsey did catch, one that was repeated was *motocicleta*. That wasn't too hard to translate.

After a while Crista turned away from the counter. She opened a drawer, removed an old-fashioned accounts book and laid it on the glass counter. She switched back to English to announce that she heard the telephone ringing in the back room and would return in a few minutes. Then she disappeared.

Rigoberto Chocron opened the accounts book and flipped pages. He stopped, fumbled in his jeans for the International Surety pen that Lindsey had given him, and for Lindsey's business card. He scribbled on the card and closed the accounts book.

Crista must have been watching, Lindsey decided, for as soon as Chocron closed the book she reappeared. Still using her excellent English, she said, 'I'm sorry, señores, that I could not be of more help. Please feel free to return to the shop any time we can be of service.'

Chocron resumed his grip on Lindsey's elbow and steered him back into the late afternoon sunlight of Calle Catorce. 'I think we need to talk.'

Lindsey waited.

'First, though, how about that five hundred dollars you owe me?'

Lindsey assented. They walked a block to a bank branch. Lindsey used an International Surety card to draw three hundred dollars from an outdoor ATM. A uniformed guard eyed them. When the transaction was completed he strode over and nodded to Lindsey.

'Everything all right, sir?' The guard looked like a Mexican to Lindsey and his accent sounded the same. Lindsey assured him that everything was all right. The guard shot a suspicious look at Chocron but didn't say anything more.

As they walked away from the bank, Chocron turned to Lindsey. 'You see that? His own kind, eh? His own kind! But he assumed you were okay. I was the gangster, just because I'm Mexican.'

'Is that why you used the name Steve Damon?'

'Of course. Who wants to read a hard-boiled murder book by some Mexican, probably an illegal? I tried Irish names, Italian names. I finally decided I'd be a pure Yankee WASP. And it worked, didn't it? So I guess it's a good name. Steve Damon, that's me.' He gestured angrily. 'Come on!' Chocron steered Lindsey toward a bar called La Puerta Amarilla, leading the way through the bright yellow door.

The place was still half empty. Lindsey figured that it would fill up soon with workers coming home from their jobs. Chocron hoisted himself onto a barstool and gestured to one next to it. Lindsey joined him there.

Chocron held out his hand. 'All right, the three hundred. And I'm going to want the other two.'

'When you earn it.' For now, Lindsey handed over five twenties. 'What was that about a motorcycle?' he asked.

'*La motocicleta?* Wow, your Spanish is improving by bounds and leaps. You must be absorbing it through your pores just from being around the barrio.'

'Very funny.'

'*Sí, amigo. Muy cómico.*'

The bartender approached and Chocron held up two fingers of one hand and pointed with the other. The bartender opened two Negra Modelos and set them in front of Chocron and Lindsey.

Chocron nodded and said, '*Pagele.*'

Lindsey found a bill in his wallet and dropped it on the dark wood. Chocron laughed and actually slapped Lindsey on the back. 'See that? Keep it up, you'll be talking like a native.' He stopped and looked around theatrically, as if expecting to be confronted by enemies. 'But if you do,' he resumed, 'you'll have to watch out for *la migra* or you'll find yourself in a bus headed back for Mexico.' He pronounced it *May-hee-co.*

Lindsey said, 'You want to go beyond that three hundred, Rigo?'

'You know it.' The jocularity had disappeared.

'I still need that computer. Now, what's this about a motorcycle?'

'Crista sold the laptop to a guy who wanted to buy a motorcycle.'

'That doesn't make sense.'

'The guy was transferring from Laney — I knew him there — Sacramento State. He was going to commute weekends.'

'From where?'

'Sacramento. I told you, he's going to Sacramento State. You see, even Mexicans know the value of education.'

Lindsey fought down an impulse to say, *Get the chip off your shoulder, Rigoberto, I'm not your enemy.* Instead he said, 'So this student is using the laptop for college work? That's what you used it for, isn't it? When you met Rachael Gottlieb?'

'Yeah.'

'How does the laptop connect with the motorcycle?'

'Don't you see? If he was going to come home every weekend and go back to Sacramento every week for classes, he needed to bring the laptop with him.'

Progress, progress. Every link in the chain led to the next link. Eventually,

Lindsey thought, he'd reach the end of the chain. The laptop. Or at least, he hoped as much.

'Give me a name.'

'The price is going up.'

'Yes.'

Lindsey watched Chocron take a sip of Negra Modelo.

'Carlos Montoya.'

'Do you know him?'

'A little.'

'You know where he lives?'

'Sure, but he wouldn't be there. He's probably in Sacramento.'

'And the laptop would be there?'

'Don't you think so?'

The bartender had furnished a pair of glasses along with the bottles of Negro Modela. Lindsey hadn't touched his beer until now. He poured it into the glass and took a sip.

'Would he have a phone there?'

'Probably. I wouldn't know the number.'

Was that it then? Had Lindsey run into a wall?

'He lives with his parents when he's in Oakland.'

Good! Chocron was looking to earn some more twenties, that was obvious. 'Would they be home now?'

'One way to find out.' Chocron finished his Negro Modela and climbed off the barstool.

The Montoya family lived on the lower floor of a cream-colored 1940s-style stucco house a few blocks from La Puerta Amarilla. Rigoberto Chocron led the way. You had to climb a short flight of stairs to reach the front door.

When Chocron rang the bell a curtain was drawn back, then allowed to fall into place again. The front door opened a crack. A gray-haired woman peered through the opening. Lindsey could see a man of the same age a few paces behind her. The woman said, '*Sí?*'

Rigoberto Chocron let out a stream in Spanish, gestured toward Lindsey, smiled and nodded at the old couple. The woman stood aside and let them in.

The living room was like a setting out of a *Three Mesquiteers* movie: overstuffed furniture, doilies on the tables and antimacassars on the chairs, family pictures on the mantel and crucifixes on the walls, a brilliant *serape* over the mantelpiece. Lindsey expected to see Duncan Renaldo ride up on his pony at any moment, or Bob Steele, or maybe even an impossibly young John Wayne.

There were portraits on the walls. Lindsey recognized a Black Madonna, *Nuestra Señora de Guadalupe*. Where in the world had he picked up that bit of information? There was a print of a stern, mustachioed Emiliano Zapata and one of a grinning, optimistic César Chávez.

Señora Montoya smiled and spoke to Lindsey in Spanish. Rigoberto Chocron said, 'She wants to know if you'd like a cup of tea. Tell her yes.'

Lindsey smiled back and said, '*Sí, gracias.*'

Señora Montoya went into a transport of delight when Lindsey spoke Spanish, however little and however poorly.

Chocron shot him an approving glance. He started a conversation with Señor Montoya. Lindsey heard Carlos Montoya's name a few times, and Sacramento, and references to *suprema*.

Señora Montoya reappeared with a tray and set it down on a table. They all shared tea and lemon cookies. Rigoberto Chocron and Lindsey thanked the Montoyas and took their leave.

Outside, walking slowly back toward Calle Catorce, Lindsey asked, 'What was that about *suprema?*'

''*Suprema?*'' Chocron burst into laughter. 'No, she wasn't saying '*suprema.*' She was saying '*su prima.*' *Dos palabras.* Two words, Mr. Lindsey. '*Su prima*' is 'his cousin.' The 'A' tells you she's a girl cousin. Carlos doesn't have the laptop anymore. He upgraded. He gave the old one to his cousin, Jade.'

'Jade,' Lindsey repeated. He managed to duplicate Chocron's pronunciation pretty well, he thought. *Jade.* Pronounced *Ha-day.*

Rigoberto Chocron said, '*Muy bien, amigo.* Same as your English word Jade, only we pronounce it differently. That beautiful green stone, you know?'

Lindsey felt complimented. He said, 'So this person, what, Carlos Montoya's cousin Jade — *Ha-day* — she has Wallace Thompson's laptop now.'

Chocron shrugged. 'I don't even know Jade. I think Carlos may have mentioned her once or twice. I think she works for a musical instrument store in Berkeley when she's not at Cal. Carlos's dad gave me her phone number.'

'All right,' Lindsey said, 'let's go see her.'

Chocron shook his head. 'Not so fast, *amigo*. I'll have to call her first and set something up. And you need to cross my palm with some more silver. You like that, cross my palm with silver? I picked that up in poetry class. Gypsies used to say that.'

Lindsey extracted another hundred dollars from the ATM on Calle Catorce. The same uniformed guard was standing outside the bank eyeballing customers as they used the machine. This time he looked twice as hard at Lindsey and Chocron, asked Lindsey again if everything was all right, and studied them as they walked away.

Chocron pulled Lindsey into the shadowed entry of a *tienda de ropas* and borrowed his cell phone to call Jade

Montoya. He chattered away in Spanish, then closed the phone and handed it back to Lindsey. He said, 'Jade is willing to talk to you. She says she has a late first class tomorrow morning; she's going to work for a couple of hours before. She wants you to come by the place where she works first. Eight o'clock. Bright-eyed and bushy-tailed, you know that expression, *amigo*?'

Lindsey slipped his cell phone back into his pocket. 'All right. What's her address?'

Chocron held out his hand. '*Tienes que cruzar mi palma con plata, amigo.*'

Lindsey didn't need a translation. He sighed and started back toward the bank. By now he felt like old buddies with the uniformed guard.

* * *

Back at his hotel room, Lindsey booted up his own laptop and keyed in a report to Richelieu. He mentioned the cash payments to Chocron and warned Richelieu that there would be more expenses before this case was settled.

He checked his pocket organizer and tapped Eric Coffman's office number in Walnut Creek into his cell phone. It was after closing time, but Lindsey knew that Eric often worked late. Even if he hadn't, there might be voicemail. But Lindsey got a recorded message saying that Coffman's number in Walnut Creek has been disconnected.

He did a little surfing and found what looked like a home listing for Eric Coffman in Emeryville. How convenient! He punched in the number and was greeted by a halfway familiar voice. He asked, 'Is this Miriam?'

'No, this is her daughter, Rebeccah. Who's calling, please? Were you trying to reach my mother?'

Good God, they did grow up, didn't they? Eric and Miriam's daughters, two little hellions in cow-ears and overalls . . . 'Yes, this is Hobart Lindsey and — '

'Just a minute, I'll get my mom.'

'No, I'm calling for — I mean, yes, I'm calling for your father, for Eric Coffman. Is he there?'

A minute later he was saying, 'Eric, I

thought that was Miriam.'

Coffman picked up the conversation as if there hadn't been a fifteen-year break. 'Miriam is fine, Bart. The girls were over for dinner tonight. Sarah has to get back to Seattle in the morning, but Rebecca lives in Oakland. We don't see them as often as we'd like. But never mind that. How are you? Where have you been hiding since the lunatics impeached Clinton? What are you up to?'

How to explain? No, there was no way. 'Just laying low, Eric. I got downsized out of I.S. I guess I was lucky at that; they twisted my arm to take early retirement. They could just have laid me off. Anyway, Ducky Richelieu called me the other day — '

'Check, check, Bart. Marston and Morse versus Gordian House, Publishers, regarding the matter of *The Emerald Cat*.'

'Right. I think we should — '

'Look, come by the office tomorrow. I'm not in Walnut Creek anymore. After the girls moved out we couldn't take it in that big house, so we're in a condo at

Watergate — you know Watergate? Talk about historical connections. And — wait a minute. Miriam's here and she wants you to come for dinner tomorrow. Yes. Right. I've got a little office in Berkeley, up in Northside. One o'clock okay? Good.' He gave Lindsey the address and hung up.

Lindsey called room service for a sandwich. He watched some news while he ate. Then he muted the TV and called Marvia Plum. This time he got through to her. She asked if he was making any progress and he said he had got on the trail of the late Gordon Simmons's missing laptop.

'You really think you've got it?'

No, he told her, no. The thing had been traded several times. But he was working on it. And what about Marvia?

She had some things to tell him, too. Maybe they could get together. How did his schedule look for tomorrow?

He made a mental note to keep his appointments with Jade Montoya at the music shop and with Eric Coffman at his office. How did late afternoon sound?

Marvia approved. BPD headquarters on Martin Luther King, four o'clock.

He'd been trudging around Berkeley and Oakland all day and his feet were sore. He finally got around to taking his shoes off. Man, that felt good! A little later, after a shower, he climbed into bed with the TV remote in his hand.

7

It was cold under the thin quilt, but Red managed to get her shakes under control by snuggling against Bobby. A jolt would have been better.

She could smell the stuff he was smoking: cheap hash, which wasn't anything that interested her much. He shook a little himself sometimes, and he didn't smell as nice to her as he used to. She could feel the tendons through his flesh. He wasn't as thin as she was, but he was getting there.

She felt him shift his weight, then push himself toward the head of the bed. She tried to ask him something and was rewarded with a whack on the back of her head. Bobby yanked the quilt off her and wrapped it around his chest.

'What's the matter, Bobby?' She pushed herself upright.

Bobby growled, 'We got any food?'

Red twisted over to the side of the bed and swung her feet onto the floor. She was already wearing two pairs of socks and she could still feel the cold. She shoved her feet into her dirty sneakers, then pushed herself upright, almost tilting over but managing to catch herself on the edge of the battered kitchen table that Bobby had found abandoned on the sidewalk and dragged back to the Van Buren and up the stairs with her help. She was proud of that, of helping Bobby get the table up to their room. It made her feel as if she was contributing to their little two-person family — that she was earning her keep; that she had a stake in their household.

There was a thin plastic take-out bag on the table. Red wasn't sure how long it had been there. At least the cold weather kept the fly population down! She opened the bag and took out a couple of Styrofoam boxes, some plastic implements, and a couple of tiny plastic condiment packets. There was a waxy cylindrical container, too, with a plastic lid, a crosshair slot in the middle and a straw through it. She hefted the container. It was halfway full.

Bobby pushed himself off the bed. He was already dressed except for his shoes.

He had a pair of old boots that he'd got out of a free box and he shoved his feet into them. He took a couple of steps to the table, pulled over one of their two rickety chairs, and slid into it.

Red waited while Bobby hefted the beverage container, sampled it via the straw, and put it on the floor next to his foot. He squinted at the Styrofoam boxes. Then he nodded, opened one, studied its contents, and opened the other. He said 'Here,' and shoved one of the boxes toward Red. It contained a half-eaten hamburger and three pickle chips.

Red picked it up and turned around, starting toward the microwave they'd salvaged off a yard sale when the owners were busy haggling with a customer over a set of cracked chinaware. But then she remembered that the microwave had gone on the fritz and there was no money to get it fixed.

'I'm sorry,' she said. She wasn't sure whether she'd said it aloud or just thought it. She was shocked to hear the dry raspy voice and the quaver in it, and told herself that it couldn't possibly have been her voice.

'Sorry for what?' Bobby asked.

So it had been her voice after all. 'Sorry the microwave doesn't work,' she managed. She felt like crying and she had no idea why that was.

'Eat your food,' Bobby said.

Red looked at his meal. It wasn't much different from hers, except whoever had abandoned it must have given up a lot sooner because there was almost a whole cheeseburger there. Bobby picked up a plastic condiment packet and opened it with his teeth. He squeezed its contents — amazingly red ketchup, the brightest stuff in their room — onto his bun. Then he dropped the packet back onto the table and started eating. Red picked up the condiment packet and coaxed another drop of ketchup onto her own burger.

When they'd eaten, Red stowed the empty Styrofoam boxes and other detritus in the plastic take-out bag and tied a knot to keep the bag from spilling. 'Bobby, Bobby honey, what are we going to do today?'

'We're headed up to Shattuck. Shattuck, Rose Street — you know the neighborhood?'

She said that she did.

'I got an idea,' Bobby told her. 'I got a great idea. I got a Plan A and I got a Plan B. Can't miss. We're gonna make some nice bread up there.'

'But . . . ' She felt herself starting to shake. She knew that Bobby didn't like it when she contradicted him, or even asked a question except what to do next. She pulled in as deep a breath as she could. 'But you told me to stick to the flatlands. That's Shattuck, Vine, that's . . . Remember what happened when I wandered up near the Claremont that time, when I slept in that guy's car — '

'Yeah, yeah, that worked out all right, didn't it? Sometimes you just get lucky. But this one I got planned. I been up there and scoped this thing out and it's win-win, bitch, it's strictly win-win.'

She nodded assent. He wasn't mad at her for questioning him. She was happy about that.

'Turn around,' Bobby said. 'Let me look at you.'

She complied.

He grunted. She tried to figure out

what the grunt meant.

He said, 'I don't know, I don't know.' He shook his head disapprovingly. 'Look at yourself. Jesus. Just look at yourself.'

She did. There was a rectangular mirror beside the door. It was pretty grimy, but it showed her herself. She looked at her face, then at her body. She began to cry. 'Bobby, what are we gonna do?'

He had an exasperated expression on his face. 'If you'd ever took care of yourself we'd be all right. But the way you look, no wonder the johns don't want you.' He took a deep breath, then went on, 'That's why we need a Plan B. You're just lucky you're with me. I'm smart; I got a Plan A and I got a Plan B.'

He crossed the room to the old dresser that came with the place, then pulled open a drawer and lifted out a couple of extra shirts that he kept there. He reached underneath the shirts and lifted something that made a sound as he moved it.

Red knew what Bobby kept in that drawer. She wasn't allowed ever to take it out, or even to pick up the shirts on top of it, or even to open the drawer. She raised one hand involuntarily to her face. She'd disobeyed Bobby once on that score, and she remembered the lesson he'd taught her about doing what he told her never to do. She still had a little sore where she'd touched that cigar lighter against her face, trying to get warm the night she got them the laptop. It was mostly healed, though, and the laptop had brought some nice money at a flea market.

Actually, Red knew, Bobby kept two things in that drawer. She knew what they were, too. She was afraid of them both. The only thing was, she couldn't decide which one she was more afraid of.

One was the knife. It was a Marine Hunter. It was eleven inches long. The blade alone was six inches long. Bobby had lifted it from a sporting goods store in Albany. They planned the lift when there was only one clerk behind the counter and no other customer in the store. It was Red's job to get the clerk's attention and keep it while Bobby made the lift.

She'd done her job. The clerk was a college kid — looked like a college kid, anyway — and Red came on to him. She had him turned away from the door, and Bobby was in and out with the knife and the clerk never even saw him. Talk about a clean lift!

The other was the gun. Red was fascinated by it. She went to the library and got online with a public-access computer and looked it up. It was something called a Beretta Stampede Thunder revolver. It was a little thing, only three and a half inches long, and it fired .357 Remington ammunition. She found one on a gun dealer's site and it was expensive.

Bobby would never tell her much about how he'd gotten the Beretta Stampede, but she managed to pry a few hints from him. A couple of big guys had been fighting it out in Oakland's Jingletown. There was some shooting, wheels, somebody had a police scanner going, and everybody got out of JT before even the first black-and-whites arrived. No, not quite everybody. A couple of bangers were dead and another one was alive but not moving, and nobody was going to stick around and try to help him.

Bobby came back from that with the

Beretta. He never told Red what he'd been doing there. The fight was strictly black on black. Whose side was Bobby on? What had he been doing there?

He told her never to touch that dresser drawer, and she never did, except when she figured she could get away with it. Then she would open the drawer and pick up the old shirts and look at the knife and the gun, and pet them.

Now Bobby took the knife out of the drawer, strapped its sheath to his belt, and closed the drawer again. 'Time to hit the street, bitch,' he said. 'You better go out and make a few dollars for us. That food wasn't too great. See if you can get something else together. Take out the garbage — you understand me?'

She nodded.

'Take out the garbage, see if you can find a couple of johns and make a few dollars. Tonight we're going out and scoring big-time.'

Red gave him the biggest, brightest smile she could muster and took out the garbage.

* * *

The Bishop Berkeley Music Shoppe must have been named in a whimsical moment, because it didn't have any of the cutesiness or cottage-in-the-glen decor that Lindsey feared he'd encounter. Instead the shop occupied the ground floor of an aging shingled house just off Ashby Avenue. The atmosphere was a mix of sixties funkiness and serious dedication to music. The place was filled with gorgeous guitars, basses, mandolins, violins, a couple of drum kits, and an assortment of horns. There was even a marvelous antique harpsichord. It must be heaven for a musician.

A young woman was standing behind the counter, wearing a dark blue Cal T-shirt and baseball cap and jeans. That seemed to be the uniform of the day, at least in this town. She was holding a brass trumpet, playing scales. There was sheet music spread in front of her. Lindsey wondered why anyone would need sheet music to practice scales, but there it was. And this gal was good.

The youngster in the Cal T-shirt spotted Lindsey and lowered the instrument. 'Can I help you, sir?'

'I hope so. Are you Jade Montoya?'

'I plead guilty. Are you here to arrest me?'

Lindsey frowned.

'Sorry, I was just kidding. I didn't mean to upset you.'

Lindsey reached for a business card and laid it on the counter, on top of the young woman's sheet music. Montoya picked up the card and studied it. Then she said, 'I guess you're not here to buy a guitar. Or are you?'

'No, I'm working on an insurance matter. Can you spare me a few minutes, Miss — '

'Just call me Jade.' She gave her name its English pronunciation. 'Would you like to sit down, sir?'

She had olive skin and glossy black hair. Her eyes were green, maybe more like emerald than jade; but still, Lindsey decided, she was well named.

'It's about a laptop computer. One that you got from your cousin Carlos.'

'Oh, no.' She put her head in her hands. 'Was it stolen? Computers seem to be the favorite target for thieves these days, more than cell phones or even guitars. Carlos has had some scrapes with the law, I'm afraid. He's always been my favorite *primo*, but I worry about him.'

Lindsey shook his head. 'Well, yes and no.'

She tilted her head like Edison's dog on the RCA Victor logo. 'I don't understand. Either the laptop was clean or it was stolen goods. How could it be both yes and no?'

'I believe your cousin got the computer from a pawnshop out in Fruitvale.'

'Okay.' She looked dubious.

'They got it — the, what do you call it, *prestamista*, a woman called Crista — she got it from a man named Rigoberto Chocron. How he got it — well, there seems to be a long, tangled trail of owners behind this thing. And, yes, I'm afraid that it was stolen at one point. But you needn't worry about that, Jade. I'm sure that your hands are clean. And your cousin Carlos — no, I don't think he has anything to worry about.'

'Well, then?'

Lindsey hesitated.

Jade Montoya glanced at an oversized wall clock, the hours indicated by musical instruments instead of numbers. At the moment it was double bass past piano. She said, 'The owner will be here in a few minutes, and I have to scamper up to the campus for Counterpoint and Composition Two-Oh-Nine.'

'There was a file on the laptop. We're quite certain it was there at the time the computer was stolen. There's likely to be a civil suit over it, an intellectual property suit. One party claims that the contents of that file — it was a novel — were published for the enrichment of a party other than the author.'

'And he's suing? Sounds reasonable enough to me.'

'Well, in fact he's deceased. But his wife's involved. And there's more. The book was contracted to a publisher, and they're threatening to sue the company that actually published the book.'

Jade Montoya's features drew back into

an impish grin. Clearly she had grasped the situation and found it amusing. 'And your role in this drama, Mr. Lindsey? Your card says you're not a police officer — you work for an insurance company.'

'International Surety needs to know whether to fight the lawsuit or to pay up.'

'Ha. Very neat.' She rubbed her slim jaw between thumb arid forefinger.

'And the computer itself is missing, is that it?'

'Precisely,' she said.

A heavyset man emerged from the back of the store. Beyond the newcomer, Lindsey could see a workshop. Disassembled instruments of various sorts were strewn across a massive workbench. The heavyset man was taller than Lindsey. He had close-cropped gray hair and wore wire-rimmed spectacles. He was carrying a tuba.

'Everything all right, Jade?' He pronounced her name in the Spanish manner.

Jade turned and handed Lindsey's card to the heavyset man. 'Remember that computer my cousin gave me a while ago? Mr. Lindsey is looking for it, for an insurance case he's working on.'

'Hardly seems worth the trouble. That thing was pretty battered. Wasn't that why you dumped it?' He didn't wait for an answer. 'Let me know when you leave so I can run the store.' He tossed a casual nod to Lindsey, turned around, and strolled back to his workshop.

'Well, I have to go to my class,' Jade said. She drew a felt-lined instrument case from beneath the counter and placed her trumpet in it. Then she folded her sheet music and slipped it into a slim portfolio.

'I still need to find that laptop,' Lindsey said.

'It crashed,' Jade Montoya said. 'For once in my life I did the sensible thing, I actually backed up my work on a flash drive. When the laptop crashed I took it to a computer store I'd heard about in Oakland to get it fixed.' She came around the counter and headed toward the street door.

Lindsey offered her a ride to the university campus and she accepted. Once in his rented Avenger, he pressed the issue. 'Congratulations on saving your data. You only saved your own files, though — not old files that were left by others?'

'I'm afraid so.'

In that case the missing file might still be found. 'Miss Montoya — Jade — what did you do with the laptop when you got it back from the computer store?'

They had reached Durant Avenue and turned up toward the University of California complex.

'I never got it back,' Jade Montoya said. 'They opened it up and told me what it would cost to get the thing up and running again and I just about fainted.'

'So — '

'So I asked them if they had a good used laptop I could buy instead and they made me an offer I couldn't refuse. So now I have a good machine. Uploaded my files and everybody goes to the beach on Sunday.'

One more important question. 'What was the name of the store?'

'Universal Data Services, Inc.'

'And what became of the old computer?'

She shrugged her shoulders. 'No idea. Maybe they junked it. Maybe they salvaged it for parts. Look, here's my stop. Thanks for the ride. Give my regards to Mrs. Columbo. Come by the store if you ever need some music.'

They stopped at Dana Street and Lindsey intended to turn anyway. He cut over to Channing, then down to Oxford, and headed for Northside.

Too early for his appointment with Eric Coffman, he found a parking spot and spent an hour happily browsing through a neighborhood bookstore. There was a pretty good section of detective novels, including a string of Tony Clydesdale pulpers by Wallace Thompson. And there was *The Emerald Cat* by Steve Damon. There was no question that the Marston and Morse titles were more attractively designed and manufactured than the Gordian House book, but a casual browser might well have taken the Damon novel for part of the Thompson series.

There was a section of used paperbacks that included a shelf and a half of old Perry Masons. Lindsey looked over a few of them, thinking more of the old Raymond Burr television series than the Gardner novels. Burr reminded him of his old friend Eric Coffman. Or the other way around. Burr was a vigorous, good-looking, athletic man in the earliest episodes. As the years went by he'd grown heavier and more ponderous, and moved more slowly; but was always confident, always in charge, always successful. And in the later color revivals he'd expanded to massive proportions, grown a beard, become nearly a parody of himself. But he was still Raymond Burr, still Perry Mason, still . . . Lindsey found himself thinking, still Eric Coffman.

The mental Rolodex popped into action. Raymond Burr. Born . . . Raymond Burr. There, at least, was a man unafraid to be who he was.

He checked the time, flipped open his cell phone, and called Eric Coffman's office.

'Bart? Where are you?'

Lindsey told him.

'For heaven's sake, you're right around the corner from here. Listen, you haven't had lunch yet, have you?'

'Matter of fact,' Lindsey said, 'I haven't really had breakfast today. I had an early appointment and I just climbed into my skivvies and headed out the door.'

'Good. Make it your breakfast, my lunch, whatever. I hope you're paying.'

Lindsey laughed.

'Look, you're at Black Oak. Meet me at Saul's. You're practically there already. Give me a minute to put my dignity back on and I'll be right over.'

8

Lindsey was engulfed in Eric Coffman's bear hug. He felt himself lifted off the ground and swung in a circle before the lawyer set him back on his feet. Coffman's big hands closed around his shoulders. Lindsey felt himself tilted back.

Coffman said, 'Okay, okay, *mein hower*, tell me how you are and what you've been up to since the age of the terrible thunder lizards. No, never mind, we need first to wrap ourselves around some good *yiddisch schpeis*. What, you're an American you and you don't speak Yiddish? You need some nourishment. First we fill the belly, and then we can talk. Come.'

Bearded now, sporting a spade-shaped Vandyke streaked with gray, and comfortable in a suit and vest that did nothing to conceal his corpulence, Coffman was either patterning himself on the latter-day Raymond Burr, or Lindsey had fallen into a TV movie.

Coffman piloted Lindsey into Saul's Delicatessen and to a table. He'd never been in the establishment before, but the sights and odors were eerily familiar. After a couple of minutes Lindsey remembered similar establishments from the one and only case that had taken him to New York, a decade and a half before.

Waiting for a waitperson to approach, Lindsey said, 'It's funny, Eric.'

'What is?'

'I was just browsing in this bookstore, looking at some Erle Stanley Gardner novels and remembering the old TV series — '

'And up shows Perry Mason in the flesh. Plenty of flesh at that, hey?' Coffman tapped a thumb against his rounded belly. 'I get a lot of that. I play into it. In my business, you need every advantage. Besides, he was a great lawyer.'

'Mason?'

'Mason? Fictitious creation. No. Erle Stanley Gardner himself. I'm glad I never had to go up against him in front of a judge. So — '

He broke off as a waitress approached.

They placed their orders.

'So, Hobart, such a long time. It's good to see you again. You're coming tonight, see our new digs.'

'You still have your little harem? I spoke with Miriam and one of the girls. They're all grown up, aren't they?'

'Alas, they try their wings and then they fly away. Sarah is married; she lives in Seattle getting rich writing software. Rebecca at least is nearby; she's teaching. In Oakland. Jingletown. Interesting neighborhood, interesting history. Some good kids in her school, some gangsters. Miriam worries.' After a pause, he added, 'I also worry. What can a father do?'

The food arrived. Lindsey looked at it and realized that he was hungry after all. He tucked in.

'So, Hobart.' Coffman took a noisy spoonful of soup. 'Officer Plum will be with you? A remarkable woman. You two were quite an item at one time. What happened? Are you totally finished?'

'I saw her a couple of days ago. She's doing well. We're friends.'

'I thought more than that. I'm

disappointed, Hobart. A fine woman. The clock is ticking, you know. You never married? Never found the right girl, or is it something else? All the years we've known each other. Is it polite to ask, even?'

That diffident Perry Mason smile, but you knew there were shark's teeth behind those smiling lips.

When they finished their meal Coffman invited Lindsey back to his office.

* * *

Coffman's office was around the corner from Saul's, half a block up Vine Street. 'Miriam encourages me to eat at Saul's,' he said. 'Climbing this hill back to my office afterwards is the only exercise I get.'

Eric Coffman and Associates was reached via a couple of clanging iron gates and an outdoor flight of stairs. It was odd architecture, but Berkeley was known as an eccentric city and its wildly varied building styles fit in with its other oddities. The office itself was spare, comfortable, and crammed with computers and other gear.

Coffman introduced Lindsey to the associates of the firm's title. There was a young law school grad of the female persuasion who went by the name of Kelly McGee, an intern, and an office manager. Coffman directed Kelly McGee to brief Lindsey on the potential *Marston and Morse v. Gordian House* lawsuit.

When the youngster finished, Coffman said, 'So, that's the legal-schmeagle stuff. What have you accomplished, my friend, playing Hawkshaw the Detective?'

Lindsey filled Coffman in on his own efforts to trace the much-traveled laptop, ending with the Bishop Berkeley Music Shoppe.

Coffman stoked his gray-flecked beard Masonically. 'So you don't have the computer? You're still pursuing it?'

'Definitely. My next stop — ' He checked his wristwatch. ' — if not today, then first thing tomorrow, is Universal Data Services, Inc.'

'Good luck with that.' Coffman shifted his weight forward in his swivel chair.

'What you tell me of this fellow Chocron makes it look pretty bad for our side. But finding the file with *The Emerald Cat* on that computer makes Chocron out to be a thief. Found property, including intellectual property, still belongs to its owner. You can't just pick it up and drop it in your pocket like a quarter on the sidewalk.

'While if we can't find it, what Mr. Chocron told you in a Fruitvale taco joint would never get into court; your statement would be pure hearsay. Chocron would have to show up and admit what he had done. And if Gordon Simmons's file — the closest thing, apparently, to an actual manuscript — doesn't turn up, then Gordian can make a different case altogether.' He leaned back again. 'I would really rather be representing Marston and Morse. Have you met Paula Paige Morse? Yes? I don't have to warn you about being careful when you talk to her. Or to Angela Simmons either. But Mrs. Morse is a lovely woman.'

Lindsey closed his pocket organizer and slipped it and his pen into his jacket pocket. He thanked Coffman for the lunch and the briefing. 'Eight tonight, your condo in Emeryville?'

Coffman pushed himself upright and shook Lindsey's hand. 'I'd walk you to your car but I've got a lot of catching up to do. Probably won't get out of here until pretty late tonight. But I'll be home for dinner.' He smiled that rueful Perry Mason smile. 'Sorry the girls won't be there, but Miriam's deeply excited. She's already working on dinner, I'm sure.'

★   ★   ★

Lindsey decided to hold off another day before talking to Universal Data Services. Instead he tried Marvia Plum's cell phone and got through on the first try.

'Bart, you making progress?'

He started to tell her but she interrupted to ask where he was. When he told her Vine at Shattuck she said, 'Listen, you're that close, come on over to my shop and we'll talk here.'

Shortly he was sharing coffee with Marvia Plum and Olaf Strombeck. He repeated essentially the same information he'd provided to Eric Coffman. When he finished his report, Marvia and Olaf Strombeck exchanged glances.

Marvia said, 'Olaf, you do the talking for us, okay?'

Strombeck nodded. 'First of all, we're interested in this matter purely as a homicide case. Mr. Simmons was killed just over a year ago. We knew that the missing laptop was in effect the murder weapon, but that was our only interest in it. The perp had been in Mr. Simmons's Chevy Malibu, presumably seeking shelter from the cold, wet weather. When Mr. Simmons approached, perp struck him with the laptop and fled.

'Okay, then this intellectual property case comes up, strictly civil, between these two publishing houses. Not particularly interesting to BPD. But Lieutenant Plum tells me that you're on the trail of the computer for reasons of your own. If you find it, then we are interested. We are very much interested.'

Lieutenant Plum. Lindsey had not seen Marvia in uniform since resuming contact. He shot her a congratulatory glance.

She responded with a wink and his pulse rate increased.

'The thing is, Mr. Lindsey, I think that you and we have started from the same point and proceeded in opposite directions.'

Lindsey frowned. 'Not sure what you mean, Sergeant.'

'You started with this fellow Burnside at Gordian House, is that correct?'

'Correct.'

'You were able to locate the missing laptop — in a sense — thanks to Mr. Chocron, and from there you've been following its trail forward.'

'Ah! I see what you mean,' Lindsey said. 'I still hope to find the computer.'

'Indeed! But now we're going to follow up with Mr. Chocron. We'll need your contact information in Fruitvale, but between the leads you've already given us — the taquería, the pawnshop, the Montoya family — I expect we'll find him.' He leaned forward. 'And once we talk to Mr. Chocron, we should be able to trace the laptop. Backtrack on its odyssey. Find out who gave it, or sold it, or swapped it to

Chocron. Or from whom he stole it. Thieves love to steal already-stolen goods. Their victims can't report the crime, you see?'

Lindsey saw.

Marvia walked to the lobby with him.

'You let Strombeck carry the ball,' Lindsey commented.

'He's a good cop. I'm planning to retire pretty soon. He's smart, honest, works hard. I'm getting him ready for my job.'

At the exit Marvia shook his hand and told him to stay in touch.

He drove back to his hotel and took a shower. He wanted to be fresh for Miriam Coffman's cooking.

★　★　★

Bobby and Red made it from Acton Street up to Northside in half an hour, alternately hiking and hitching rides. The last ride was a blast. Dude in a slate-gray ragtop Beamer. Had the stereo on loud blasting punk rap all the way. Dropped them right at the corner of Shattuck and Vine and blasted off, headed toward the Solano Tunnel, El Cerrito, Vancouver, and the North Pole.

'Give my regards to Santy, you sucker!' Bobby called after the Beamer. The driver waved a friendly good-bye. Probably hadn't heard what Bobby had said. Before the ragtop disappeared, Bobby read the vanity license plate. BMRMEUP.

'I wish we had a car,' Red said. 'Wouldn't it be great to have a car like that one? We could just go cruising around, music on the stereo, maybe stop for a jolt every so often. I'd never come down, Bobby. Never come down. Think of that! Stay jolted forever and ever and ever and ever and ever.'

She stopped when he grabbed her by both arms and shook her, hard. That was okay, it was okay, it was better than getting hit, it was okay.

'Now listen,' Bobby hissed. 'Pay attention!' It was dark out now. Illumination came from the headlights of passing cars and in the little restaurants on the other side of Shattuck.

Bobby thought that if Red didn't get her act together, he was going to have to get rid of her. And soon. He needed a bitch and Red just wasn't cutting it anymore. She couldn't snag the johns; she was just too scrawny and strung out. She scared 'em away instead of hauling 'em in. She wasn't even any good to Bobby himself. He needed to replace her.

He looked at the little office building halfway up Vine toward Walnut. 'Look at that place.' He took her head in his hands and turned her so she had to see the upstairs light. 'Do you see that?'

She managed to stammer an answer.

'All right.' Bobby sat down next to her. There was a public bench there on the sidewalk, on the same side as the office building, facing the little mall. He leaned in close and put his arms around her. Anybody walking past would take them for a couple of kids: a bony, hot-to-trot girl and her on-the-make boyfriend.

'Now listen. There's an old guy works up there. I've been up here before; I've seen him. He's old and he's fat and he can hardly move, he's so decrepit. He likes to work late and then leave. Now look, we can see the light in his place from here. When he turns it out, he comes down those outside stairs and through that iron gate. He parks his car in a garage up on Walnut. Are you with me, you brainless shit?'

'Yes,' she whispered.

'As soon as he turns off the light, we beat it up the hill. We'll be past that gate before he's even halfway down the stairs. We get to the corner up there. When he turns to go get his car on Walnut, you come up in front of him. Give him a come-on. These ancient guys, they all have crazy ideas about making it with younger women, you understand?'

She nodded, eager to please. 'Yes, Bobby.'

'If he goes for it, you get him a little further away from the people on Vine and I'll come from behind. We should be able to take him for everything he's got. Money, BlackBerry, whatever the hell he's got.'

'Bobby, I'll try. I'll do my best. But what if he doesn't go for it?'

'Don't worry about that, bitch. Just do your job, and if anything goes wrong I'll take care of it.'

'Okay.'

'Look, look up there. The light just went out. Get a move on, now!'

★ ★ ★

Eric Coffman used his BlackBerry to phone Miriam and tell her he was on his way. He was on Vine Street already, almost at the corner, and would be in the car and on the way in five minutes.

Seeing Hobart Lindsey again had been a pleasure, and having him to the Emeryville condo for dinner would be more of the same. The case of *Marston and Morse v. Gordian House* was more of a detective story than a legal problem. If it ever even happened. He knew Hobart Lindsey; knew that the pleasant-demeanored, sometimes almost timid one-time claims adjuster was in fact a highly effective investigator. He was something of a plodder, but his closure rate was better than that of many a flashier operative.

He'd turned the corner onto Walnut, his legs on autopilot, his mind on other matters, when something warm and

148

fleshy bounced off his chest. He let out a startled gasp.

'Watch out, Mister! Don't you — '

There wasn't much light just here, but Coffman could see that he'd collided with a young girl. She was skinny, wore a Berkeley High T-shirt, and had short-cropped red hair. He started to apologize, but before he could get past a stammered word or two she was patting him on the shoulder, peering up into his face, actually smiling at him.

'I know you didn't mean it, sir.' She touched his cheek softly and ran her hand through his beard. 'I like men with beards,' she said. He wasn't sure whether her smile was attractive or not. Her features were certainly pretty. In the faint light of Walnut Street it was hard to tell. But there was an unhealthy look to her. He suppressed a shudder.

She said, 'Are you busy right now? You look like you might enjoy . . . ' She left it there.

'Are you all right, miss?' he asked her. 'There are some restaurants nearby. Have you had your dinner?' He reached for his wallet and started to extract a couple of bills. He extended them toward the girl, then looked at her more closely. 'Listen, how old are you?'

'Never mind that, grandpa!' She grabbed the bills and looked at them, then said angrily, 'You can do better than that! Picking on children. You belong in jail. Stop it! Let me go!'

She was screaming now. Around him, Coffman could see movement inside lit windows, figures rushing to see what was going on. He felt a thump on the back of his head, then a sharp pain in his back, then saw redness, then blackness.

Bobby pulled his prized Marine Hunter out of the old guy's back. The guy was lying on his face, bleeding though his suit jacket. Bobby held up the blade, then bent over and wiped it carefully on the old guy's back, once, twice, then returned it to its sheath.

Red was dancing around, chattering like a monkey. Bobby jumped to his feet and hit her once in the face with his fist. She stopped dancing around and chattering and stood there with her hands in front of her mouth. She looked like she was getting ready to cry, but Bobby didn't have time to waste on her. People were coming from the buildings and he had to get out of there.

Where the hell was the old guy's wallet? Right, there it was — a couple of feet away, lying on the sidewalk. Bobby picked it up, then turned back to the old guy. He was wearing a nice-looking wristwatch on a metal expansion band. That was good. The watch came off easily. He probably had a cell phone and maybe some other valuables, but there was no time to look for those.

Bobby ran up Walnut Street, away from the coffee-guzzlers and the yuppies. The further you got from Vine, the darker it got. That was good. Bobby was young and in good shape — well, pretty good shape, and he had a head start.

He could hear Red's voice. She was behind him, running as fast as she could, but she wasn't as fit as he was and for a moment he thought he might just let her get caught. That way he would be rid of her without having to do anything nasty to her himself. But then the cops would have her and she'd babble, he knew she'd babble, and cops would wind up at Acton Street. He'd never be able to go back there. And the Beretta Stampede Thunder revolver was there; he didn't want to risk losing the Beretta.

So he turned around, actually ran a few steps back toward the pursuers, grabbed Red by the wrist and tugged her after him, running toward Rose Street. There were yards and shrubs around the houses up there, and a little further a big park full of rolling hills. If they could get that far, he was pretty sure they'd be all right.

He'd still be stuck with Red, but they would have the old guy's wallet with cash in it, and credit cards they could maybe use or maybe sell. And there was that fancy wristwatch.

9

Strombeck was there and barely blinked when Lindsey came pounding into the waiting room at Alta Bates. With Strombeck was Marvia Plum and one of Eric Coffman's daughters. This had to be Rebecca, the one who taught school in Jingletown. She was sitting with her mother, her arms around her, nodding her head and murmuring things that Lindsey couldn't make out.

Lindsey braced Strombeck. 'What the hell happened? I was just up there. I ate lunch with Eric today — we had a meeting at his office this afternoon. What happened to him?'

'Looks like a mugging gone wrong, Mr. Lindsey. We'll know better when we can talk to Mr. Coffman.'

'He's going to be all right, then?'

'Have to ask the docs. It looks as if the perp hadn't planned this. He got panicky and ran away. Didn't stay around to finish the job.'

'Why would anyone want to kill Eric Coffman?'

'We'll have to find out. As I said, I think it was a mugging. Probably a two-man job that went wrong.'

'Why two-man?'

'So far, there appears to be a single wound. Well, two if you count a thump on the back of the head. But that doesn't look serious. There was a sharp-instrument wound in the victim's lower back. That *is* serious. His wallet and wristwatch are missing. Now, why would a mugger attack his victim from behind? Not good technique. They usually work face-to-face. So in all likelihood there were two perpetrators, working as a team. We've had a rash of these lately.' For a moment the unflappable Olaf Strombeck turned human. His face scrunched up as if he was exhausted but determined to keep going. He rubbed his eyes with a huge hand.

A doctor came into the room. 'Is Mrs. Coffman here?'

Miriam Coffman turned and raised one hand like a schoolchild answering a roll call. Her daughter Rebecca kept her arm around her.

'I am Dr. Pollyam Mukerji. I have just been with Mr. Coffman. I am the surgeon on duty tonight.'

The doctor huddled with the two other women. The scene was classic, but the gown was green instead of white, and the surgeon should have been Lew Ayres or Lionel Barrymore or Richard Chamberlain. Instead this surgeon was an Indian woman, dark-skinned and petite, with a red dot on her forehead and a glossy braid hanging behind her. She wore wire-rimmed granny glasses.

Dr. Mukerji nodded, and the two Coffman women disappeared through the doorway. Then she repeated her self-introduction to the others. Now she was talking to Lieutenant Plum, Sergeant Strombeck and Hobart Lindsey. 'You are . . . ?'

They gave their names.

'Very well. Mr. Coffman received a very serious knife wound. The knife entered his body from behind, passing beneath his rib cage. There was considerable damage to his liver, pancreas, and stomach. Several blood vessels were severed. There was a small insult to the bottom of the right lung. There was no damage to the heart. There is no apparent nerve damage. The patient will remain in guarded condition for at least a day, but I anticipate a good recovery.'

Marvia Plum asked if Coffman was conscious. Dr. Mukerji said he was not. When would he regain consciousness? Probably in one to two hours. Could they speak with him then? Briefly. His wife and daughter were with him now.

When Dr. Mukerji left, Lindsey sat down with Marvia and Olaf Strombeck. Marvia said, 'Rebecca asked me to call you. She said Miriam insisted. You were supposed to come for dinner and she didn't want to stand you up.'

That evoked a dour expression from Lindsey. 'How did Eric wind up here? How did they even know who he was?'

'Fair enough question,' Strombeck replied. 'The muggers got his wallet but they left his BlackBerry. The cover was broken when he hit the sidewalk but the innards still work. It was easy to trace his ID from that. We sent a unit to Watergate to fetch Mrs. Coffman. She asked us to call the daughter.' He paused. 'And the dinner guest.'

'What was your meeting with Coffman about?' Marvia asked.

'This Gordian House copyright problem. I don't see why — '

'Looks unconnected,' Strombeck said. 'But still . . . do you think somebody wanted to kill Mr. Coffman? That the whole mugging incident was a cover?'

'I don't know,' Lindsey said.

'First lesson I ever learned from Dorothy Yamura,' Marvia was saying. ' "There really are such things as coincidences, but they make me nervous.' Maybe this really is a coincidence. But maybe it isn't.'

Lindsey promised to drop in at police headquarters the next day to give a formal statement. 'Do you think the other people at that meeting in Eric's office should come in, too?' That was his last question of the night.

The answer from Strombeck was, 'Probably not. Not right now, anyway.'

Lindsey went back to his room at the Woodfin and ordered a sandwich and a pot of coffee from room service. He chewed and swallowed and sipped and didn't taste anything.

★   ★   ★

Lindsey had spent the night dozing and waking, the faces of the characters in this weird charade swirling overhead like soap bubbles circling the drain in a bathtub. By morning he was still far from a solution, but at least he felt that the pieces were starting to fall into place. He connected his laptop to the internet and sent a report to Richelieu in Denver.

He grabbed a Danish and a glass of apple juice, retrieved his Avenger, and drove to Berkeley Police Headquarters. There he picked up his visitor's badge again and waited for an escort to a cramped conference room. As he made his way down the grim hallway, he glanced through a window into an office where a middle-aged couple were in earnest conversation with a female police officer.

158

Once in Sergeant Strombeck's perfectly ordered office, Marvia Plum sat in on the meeting, but she let Strombeck do the work.

*　*　*

Ironically, a conversation was going on in another office a few doors away that might have had an important impact on the meeting concerning Eric Coffman. Nobody knew. Nobody knew.

Officer Celia Varela had been through this kind of conference a hundred times before, but it never failed to wrench her guts and challenge her professionalism. Sometimes she felt more like a social worker than a cop. Maybe she should be out there shooting at crooks, bringing in bad guys, and locking them in cells. But this was cop work, too. Finding missing people. Especially missing children. Missing and Exploited Children — that was the unit's name. And working there would break your heart if you let it.

The couple facing her couldn't have been more than forty, but the stress lines in their faces and the alternate white knuckles and trembling hands made them seem far older. 'I'm really sorry, Mr. and Mrs. Horton,' Officer Varela said, 'but I don't think I have anything new to give you today. We're working on the case constantly. The trouble is, we don't even know if Rebi is still in Berkeley. Many of these children are runaways. A lot of them turn up in Los Angeles, but others are found in New York, Chicago, Seattle. Or — well, anywhere in the world.'

'And the ones who don't turn up at all?' The father's hair was iron-gray.

'I'm sorry,' Varela said. How many times had she heard herself saying that? 'The majority do turn up, and we send them back to their families. I wouldn't give up. We're still looking for Rebi, and when we find her — '

'You did find her!' This time it was the mother who interrupted. 'You found her and you sent her to that juvenile hall place. What a name for that dungeon! It sounds like something out of a Disney movie. It's nothing but a prison and a crime school for children. It's Guantanamo.

It's Abu Ghraib. It — '

Her husband put his hand over her mouth. 'Stop!'

She clawed his hand away with both of hers. 'Where is she? I want my daughter!'

Celia Varela was halfway out of her chair when she saw that Mr. Horton had got his wife under control. She slumped into her chair, pulled a handkerchief from her purse — a Versace original, and sobbed into it. Her husband sat with his hand on her back, looking at Varela, breathing deeply.

When Mrs. Horton regained control of herself she said, 'You know, you did have her.'

Varela looked down at the case folder on her desk. 'We did find her. The court sent her to juvenile hall. And she was returned to you.'

'And promptly disappeared again!'

'Yes, ma'am.'

Now Dad spoke up. 'We gave her everything. We enrolled her in the finest private schools. She refused to attend. We tried to send her out of state to a boarding school. She refused to go to the airport.

We tried to bribe her. Nothing. She just wanted to go to public school and be with her so-called friends. Criminals and degenerates. Criminal degenerates. That says it all. Criminal degenerates.'

'The public schools turn out many fine people,' Celia said.

Dad said, 'Have you any clues?'

Mom said, 'She was only home for a few hours. We picked her up at that awful place and brought her home for a good scrubbing. She was filthy, and we dressed her in a beautiful outfit and we took her out for a special meal to celebrate her homecoming. We didn't criticize, we didn't condemn.'

Dad made a humming sound.

'All right, I might have said a couple of words. And if *he* had taken responsibility and not treated his daughter like a royal princess who could do no wrong, his little angel . . . '

'Please, Carolyn.'

'All right, never mind. I won't try to place blame. I just want my daughter back. I want her home with her family. So we took her to Chez Panisse. Alice Waters personally greeted us. We've been family friends for decades. And it was a wonderful meal. The service was perfect. And we came home, and she said she was happy to be home but she was tired and wanted to go to bed.' She paused for breath, then plunged on. 'And not an hour later, I went to check on her and she was gone again. Gone, after all that. You know, we had special locks on the doors and the windows so she couldn't sneak out at night, and they didn't stop her. Eat dinner, go upstairs, gone. Gone. And now where is she?'

'That's what we're trying to find out, Mrs. Horton.' Celia Varela steeled herself for what she knew was coming next.

Mr. Horton started the standard rant about his taxes and her badge. She held her tongue until it was time for her next appointment, this one with a woman whose husband had absconded and taken their toddler, two beagles, and a parakeet with him.

Once the Hortons left, she heaved a sigh and opened another case folder.

*　*　*

A few doors away, just a few doors away, Marvia Plum and Olaf Strombeck and Hobart Lindsey had gone over what was known of the previous day's activities involving Eric Coffman. Officer Jo Rossi was invited into the conference. She had gone up to Coffman's office on Vine Street and recorded brief statements from his young associate, his legal intern, and the office manager. Rossi had even stopped in at Saul's Delicatessen and tracked down the waitress who had served them. Everything checked out against Lindsey's version; not that there was any reason to expect otherwise.

'Just between us,' Marvia said as she stood up, closed the door, and sat down again, 'what do you think about the Coffman case and the Simmons homicide? Come on, the tape is turned off; nobody's going to come back at you for stating an opinion.'

'Put me down for Yamura's Law, Lieutenant.' Strombeck had not hesitated.

'Bart?'

'I want to know more.' He stood up angrily. 'In the present case, we just have to keep on digging. Digging and digging. Until we hit paydirt.'

'Do think there's a key to this whole mess?'

'You bet there is,' Strombeck said. 'It's that goddamned computer.'

'I've been looking for it since I started work on this,' Lindsey said. 'I think I'm getting close.'

Marvia said, 'You're going in the wrong direction, Bart. Wrong for us. Right for you, I suppose. You want the computer itself, right?'

'That's right. So I can see if Simmons's novel is on it. The one that Chocron gave a thin coat of shellac and sold to Gordian House as his own.'

'Olaf, you and I need to go in the opposite direction. Track it back to that dark and stormy night when it was stolen from Gordon Simmons's Chevy. That's how we'll unravel this thing.' She paused, hot and bothered. 'And I'll bet a week's pay that when we do that, we'll also crack the Coffman attack.'

10

'Should I clear out?' Lindsey asked.

'Why?'

'Well, you're planning police tactics and I'm a civilian.'

'Stay. Sit. You're part of this thing. You know procedure, Bart. And we need your input on this.'

Strombeck said, 'I should head down to Fruitvale and get started on this, Lieutenant. Should probably go in civvies.'

Marvia gave forth with the grin that Lindsey had loved for so long. 'No, I don't think so.'

'Reason, Lieutenant?'

'Nothing like a six-foot-something blond Viking named Olaf to blend right in, in Fruitvale where the average male is about five seven and barely able to pass the brown-bag test. No, Olaf, this one is mine.' She stood up. 'I'll contact the Oakland gang unit and let them know I'm coming. If I'm lucky and I need some help, they'll give it. In any case, they're less likely to shoot me.'

She reached for a couple of case folders on Strombeck's desk, pulled a pad from her own pocket, and jotted notes. Even in a Buck Rogers world the pencil and paper survived.

'Okay, Bart, let's review. Your man is one Rigoberto Chocron, a.k.a. Steve Damon. No permanent address or phone number. Best chance of contact is through a restaurant called Los Arcos de Oro on Foothill Boulevard in Fruitvale.'

'That's it. But . . . wait a minute.' Lindsey fumbled for his cell phone. He opened the clamshell and retrieved the picture he'd snapped of Rigoberto Chocron as Chocron arrived at Los Arcos de Oro.

Marvia had the phone out of his hand before he could lose the image. 'Hobart, this is great. Olaf, get this over to I.T. and have 'em load it into the system. And get some printouts. Lindsey, spell! Spell! This guy's name, his Anglo handle, that restaurant, name and address, and the phone number there.'

Lindsey spelled. Strombeck disappeared.

Marvia shook her head. 'Bart, you are either the world's greatest detective or a complete nincompoop. Getting Chocron's photo was brilliant. Either way, I . . . never mind.'

Lindsey blinked. 'Call me Maxwell Smart. Or maybe Jacques Clouseau.'

'I'll just stick to Hobart Lindsey, thanks.'

While Strombeck was at I.T., Marvia asked Lindsey what he was going to do next.

'I'm going to talk to the people at Universal Data Services. Hobart Lindsey, computer detective, hot on the case of the little lost laptop.' He paused. 'Marvia, what about Eric Coffman?'

'I spoke with Dr. Pollyam Mukerji this morning. She confirms Mr. Coffman will make a good recovery. He's going to be in intensive care for a couple of days and then they're going to keep him in Alta Bates for a week at least, sitting up there on the fifth floor watching the red-tailed hawks playing in the tall pines.'

'Visitors allowed?'

'They try to keep it down to family but I think you could get in. Call his wife first. Or, no, I imagine she's at his bedside now.'

'Did you get anything out of him?'

She smiled again, but not that wonderful glowing smile. More like a cat-who-ate-the-canary smile. 'You got it. I was over there again this morning. You know they get people up early in the hospital to make sure they got plenty of sleep. Mr. Coffman was sitting up and grousing to beat the band because he doesn't have any appetite this morning.'

'Is that bad news?'

'Mr. Coffman thinks it is. Dr. Mukerji says he's lucky to be alive. You wouldn't think it from the wound — she showed me pictures — but if that knife had gone a couple of inches more in practically any direction, he'd be in much worse trouble than he is. Either that, or on a slab.'

'Did Eric remember anything useful? Did the attacker say anything?'

'Coffman says he was approached by a very young woman. Hardly more than a little girl. He took her for a panhandler and he pulled out his wallet to give her some money. That's when her confederate hit him from behind.'

'But why stab him? If it was a mugging and Eric already had his wallet out . . . hitting him on the head, that sounds like the sucker punch tactic. But why the knife attack?'

'Here's why. The way Coffman describes the girl, she's almost certainly a junkie of some sort. Most likely a meth freak. She was supposed to do a poor-hungry-waif act, or maybe a sexual come-on. Either plain garden-variety prostitution, or more likely entrapment and extortion.'

'A badger game.'

'Right.'

Strombeck got back from I.T. and slipped into the room. Lindsey asked, 'What went wrong?'

'The girl is a freak, Hobart. Who knows how high she was flying. Or maybe she was crashing. All the more desperate. She goes into her act, the john doesn't respond the way she expected, or maybe she just forgets her lines and freaks out. The john starts to back away and the girl's boy-friend figures, we don't want to let this one get away, he's too juicy.' Strombeck laid some papers on his desk, reached a long uniform-clad arm toward Lindsey, and returned his cell phone.

'So, the wallop on the back of the head,' Marvia resumed. 'Doc Mukerji says Coffman was lucky on that score, too. She doesn't think the perp used a sap. More likely a hard, heavy object, probably a potato-sized rock that the perp picked up right at the scene. A little harder and Coffman could have gone down with a crushed skull and brain trauma. Instead, he's got a concussion and he'll have headaches for a while, but he should be all right.'

'Then why the knife?' Lindsey asked.

'You want these creeps to make sense? If the girl panicked and forgot her lines, then her partner might have done the same. He's dangerous. Violent. That's assuming the girl's partner was a boy. Might have been a two-girl team. Gender equality is real big in Berkeley.'

Nobody laughed.

'He might have planned a simple mugging, but nobody made him carry that knife with him,' Marvia continued. 'If he'd left the knife at home . . . well, he might still have clouted Coffman with the rock, there's no telling, but when we catch the thug that knife will go against him. Big time. He might have grabbed the rock and hit Coffman in a moment of panic, but he brought that knife with him. That's premeditation. We'll get the creep, and that will be important when we take the case over to the DA.'

She stood up. 'Enough. We can sit here and play Clue all day, but the only way to catch the bad guys is to go out and grab 'em by the ear and drag 'em to the principal's office.'

Lindsey said, 'Fair enough. I'll go pay a visit to Alta Bates, and then I'm off to Universal Data Services in Oakland.'

'Good. You keep chasing that computer. But listen, that's not just a piece of evidence in your civil case. It's a murder weapon. I'm sending an officer with you. Strombeck, hunt up Jo Rossi. She's smart, and she needs to get out of the shop and back on the street.'

Lindsey did not protest.

* * *

Marvia Plum scampered back to her own office and got on the horn to OPD gang unit. She reminded them of who she was — they were not strangers — and told them what she was planning to do. The duty officer at OPD asked if she wanted a partner or backup. She said no, she was only investigating at this point.

Before she left BPD headquarters, she checked out Steve Damon and came up dry. That was no surprise. She tried Rigoberto Chocron and discovered that he'd entered the country legally on a student visa and enrolled at Laney College in Oakland. He'd dropped out of Laney and his student visa had been cancelled. He was eligible for deportation but had dropped off the radar, and *la migra* had no idea where he was. Still, he was hardly a high priority ICE target. He was one of the 12 million most wanted illegals in the country.

Thanks be to the Goddess Justitia for zapping a brainwave to Hobart Lindsey and getting him to snap that cell phone shot of Chocron. It was hardly portrait quality, but it was good enough to give Marvia an idea of what Chocron looked like. And another break — apparently Rigoberto Chocron was his real name.

She used the voluminous pockets of a loose-fitting padded jacket to carry her equipment. She stopped at Dorothy Yamura's office on her way out of the building. When she explained her mission to Captain Yamura, Yamura asked how she hoped to get Chocron to talk, assuming that she was able to find him.

'From Hobart Lindsey's report, Chocron is amenable to a little cash persuasion.'

Yamura looked pensive. 'That's a dangerous tactic.'

'Do you have another suggestion?'

After a moment of contemplation, Yamura said, 'Yes, I have.' She explained her idea and Marvia reacted enthusiastically. As Marvia left Yamura's office, Yamura was reaching for the telephone.

* * *

Lieutenant Plum revved up her souped-up Falcon and headed for Oakland. She found a parking place on Foothill Boulevard and strolled into Los Arcos.

A smiling Mexican man gestured her toward a table, but she stopped him and asked if he spoke English. His reply indicated that his linguistic skills were even more limited than her own, but she managed to get a message across.

'*Busco a Rigoberto Chocron. Está aquí?*'

The man smiled at her Spanish. He shook his head and shrugged. '*No está. No le conozco.*' No, he didn't know him but he knew he wasn't here.

'*Chocron usa su teléfono, no es verdad?*'

'*No, señora, no tenemos un teléfono.*'

Right. She believed that absolutely, and by the way, did Los Arcos happen to have a nice big *puente* they'd like sell? She could set up tollbooths and get rich that way.

The trouble was, as far as she knew, Chocron wasn't wanted for anything except an immigration complaint, and that was a *muy* low priority. You could smoke pot on the police HQ lawn if you really wanted to get arrested, before any Berkeley or Oakland cop would hassle you over a *migra* beef.

No point in staking out Los Arcos in hopes of finding Chocron. At least at this point. She told the man '*Grácias*' and went on her way.

At the pawnshop on East Fourteenth Street, she stopped and studied the contents of the window. As she walked in she spotted a shape disappearing into the back of the store. Nothing she could do about that. The woman behind the counter was obviously the *prestamista*, exactly as Hobart Lindsey had described her.

Marvia faced her. '*Señora Crista?*'

'*Sí.*'

'*Habla el Ingles?*'

'*Poco.* Do you speech the Spanish?'

'*Poquito.*'

'Okay, then. Let's use English, okay? What do you want? You come here to pawn something or to buy something?'

'Neither. I just need to ask you a couple of questions.'

'You're a real cop. You not *la migra*. I can smell them a mile away.' She held her nose. 'Regular cops smell different from *la migra*. I didn't smell you until you came into my store. What do you want? You OPD? You looking for stolen goods? I don't take stolen goods.'

This lady was pretty sharp. In her line of work it made sense. 'I saw some computer equipment in your window. I'm trying to find a laptop computer.'

'We get them sometimes. I don't think we got any right now.'

'I'm looking for a particular one. You might have had it and then the owner redeemed it or you sold it.'

'When would that be? You know when that would be, when you think we maybe had it? You got a serial number? Brand? What?'

Marvia flipped to her notebook. So much for blending into the community. She hadn't identified herself as an officer, but *Crista-la-prestamista* didn't need her to do that. She read the data she'd gotten from the Simmons case file.

Crista pursed her lips. She shot a

177

glance toward the back room; from her side of the counter Marvia could not see who or what was back there. She said, 'I'll have to go look it up. We have to keep records, you know, it's the law.' She paused, but Marvia did not take the bait.

Crista disappeared. There was the sound of hushed conversation from the back. For a moment Marvia considered circling the counter and confronting Crista and whoever she was talking with. It might even be Rigoberto Chocron himself. Lindsey had said that Chocron and Crista were acquainted. He wasn't sure how chummy they were — at one point, Crista was treating Chocron as a casual acquaintance, but then again Lindsey described Chocron doing his Latin lover act on the woman.

The woman reappeared. 'Maybe I can help you. Maybe I'm not so sure. Why did you say you want this computer?'

'For starters, it was stolen.'

'Recently?'

'No. A year ago, a little more.'

'So why you looking for it now? What could it be worth? Maybe a few dollars?

Maybe even a hundred dollars? These things, they keep changing them, don't they? This one you're looking for, why you even care anymore?'

'Crista, this particular laptop was involved in at least one very serious crime. Completely aside from the original theft.'

'And you think you know who did this thing?'

'Who was that in the back room you were talking to?'

'Just the janitor. He came to take out the trash from the store.'

'I don't think so.'

'All right, so maybe he don't have any green card. You gonna bust him?'

Marvia shook her head. 'I told you, I'm not ICE, I'm not *la migra*. I don't care if he's from Mexico or Mars. I'm not going to arrest him.'

'But you a cop, right? I told you, cops have a smell.'

'Okay, I'm a cop. But all I want right now is some information, and I think your friend can help me.'

'What you want from him?'

'He brought the computer in here and pawned it, didn't he? Did he redeem it, or did you sell it to somebody else?'

'What's the difference? It's gone. I don't have it no more.'

'Señora, what I need to know now is how the person who pawned it got it. That was Rigoberto Chocron, wasn't it? Is Rigoberto here? He's the person you were talking with. He's not in trouble, I promise. I just need to talk to him.'

'Oh, I understand. A cop would never tell a lie, right? You wait here for a minute.'

She disappeared again, then returned. 'Nobody back there. I guess the janitor finish his work and leave. He not a very reliable character, you know?'

This was not going well. If Marvia tried to lean on Crista, that would be the end of any chance from this angle. 'Okay, look, suppose I give you my contact information.' She produced her card and slid it across the glass countertop.

Crista picked it up and studied it. She said, 'You wait here a little longer.' She disappeared once more and — surprise!

— Rigoberto Chocron appeared in her place. Lindsey had done a good job with his cell phone. This was definitely the guy.

Chocron said, 'Why you so interested in that laptop computer? I used it for school. I didn't like the course. It was women's poetry. I thought it might be kind of, you know, maybe romantic. But it was mainly about hating men and women loving other women. Not my kind of stuff, you know? So I hocked the thing. I was gonna come back for it but I didn't really need it, so I just left it.'

'Mr. Chocron — ' He seemed startled that she knew his name. For a moment she feared that he was either going to bolt or attack her. But he waited, poised. She could read the fight-or-flight tropism ready to go either way. 'Señor Chocron,' she tried again, 'I'm sure you heard my conversation with Crista.'

He nodded.

'I'm not after you. I'm trying to backtrack the trail of that computer. I only came here to find out who Crista got it from. Now if you could tell me who you got it from, I'd be one step closer to catching a really bad person.'

'How bad?'

'A killer.'

'Gang stuff? I don't get involved in no gang stuff. That's much too dangerous, too many people get killed. Mexicans, blacks, we kill each other, nobody cares. You're pretty black, lady, you ought to know that. Somebody white must of got killed. Is that it?'

'I can't go into that. I can only promise you I'm not after you. You're just a link in a chain and I have to keep going.'

'A link, hey?' He nodded and ran his fingers across his face. He was actually handsome in a fast-moving, elusive kind of way. 'You wearing a wire?'

'No,' Marvia said. 'I'll level with you. I am carrying communication equipment but it's turned off. And I am armed, yes. But I don't expect to use any force today. I really just want to talk.'

He considered. Then, 'All right. Hold on.' To Crista, a staccato burst of Spanish that Marvia couldn't begin to follow, but the response was clearly positive.

Chocron gestured toward the curtained

area and Marvia followed him into the back room. It was dusty and cluttered, with a few chairs and a table and a microwave.

Chocron gestured. 'Sit down.'

She did.

'Ask.'

'When did you obtain the computer? Where? How? From whom?'

'I bought it.'

'Really? Did you know it had been stolen?'

'No. I bought it at a flea market.'

'Where?'

'I don't remember. There a lot of flea markets around here. People not so rich, you know?'

'I understand. But I want you to try and remember. It's not like you buy a computer every day.'

'That's for sure. But she told me I need one.'

'Who did?'

'My poetry professor. Professor Rosemary Rostum.'

'Did she tell you where to get it?'

'Not exactly.'

'Come on, Rigo, you can do better than

that. Look, I just need a little more information and I'll leave you alone. And I promise, not a word to ICE.'

'Okay, I got it at that flea market out near the coliseum.'

'By the freeway there?'

'That's the one. An old drive-in movie place. You can get some good stuff there.'

'You remember the name of the vendor?'

He shook his head.

'Did you get a receipt?'

'Yes. You need it to get out of there. They're afraid of shoplifters . . . but I didn't save it,' he added.

Marvia sighed. 'Would you recognize the vendor if you saw him or her again? Was it a man or a woman?'

'It was a man. A white guy.'

'Age?'

'Oh, I don't know. How you expect me to remember some dude I met once half a year ago and never saw again no more?'

'Please try.'

Chocron closed his eyes and put his hand to his forehead. Then, 'He had gray hair and a ponytail; he was maybe fifty. Heavy guy. Big shoulders, big belly, wore a Space Cadet baseball cap with his ponytail pulled through it.'

'He wore a *what* kind of baseball cap?'

'Space Cadet. It had a picture of a rocket ship and a planet on it and it said 'Space Cadet.' And I remember now, there was two of them. What a couple of characters. Mister and Missus Space Cadet. I remember them now.'

'Mr. Chocron, would you recognize these people if you saw them again?'

'I don't know. I guess so.'

'If I take you with me to the flea market this Sunday, do you think you could point him out to me?'

'I don't know. He didn't give me no hassle, didn't demand ID or nothing. I don't want to get him in trouble.'

'You won't get him in trouble, really. You've been very helpful. I told you, this works like a chain. Mr. Space Cadet is the next link in the chain.'

Chocron stared at Marvia Plum. She stared back.

'What's in it for me, Madame Cop?'

'A green card.'

'You know I overstayed my last one.'

'I'm talking about immigrant status, not student.'

'You're a local cop. You don't give out green cards. Who do you think you're kidding?'

'You're right, Rigoberto. We don't have green cards to give out, but we have connections with *los federales*, you understand that? Believe me. You'll have a green card in your hand if you help me. Otherwise — I gave you my word I would still not blow the whistle on you, no *migra* problems, but no green card, either.'

'Meet me at Los Arcos *esta Domingo a las diez por la mañana*. And *desayuno* is on you, right?'

Marvia stuck out her hand and Rigoberto Chocron shook it.

*   ★   ★

The Hortons had an early dinner. They left the dishes on the table. They knew they would be cleared and washed and put away. One advantage of having money was that you didn't have to worry about things like doing the dishes or folding the laundry.

Not that they were the children of privilege and wealth. Joe Horton had built a business from nothing. And Carolyn had been with him every step of the way, holding down menial jobs as a young wife to help fill the family coffers, then staying home to care for their daughter without benefit of day care or babysitters.

Now they had plenty of money, a big house, two new cars.

They had nothing.

Joseph Horton looked at his watch and nodded. This time of year, the evenings were short. He said, 'I'm going out.'

'Looking?' It was only half a question.

'Of course. Want to come along?'

'No . . . not tonight. I think I'll just stay home and . . . I don't know. I'll just stay home.'

'All right,' he said.

'Where will you go?'

'I think MacArthur in Oakland. Or maybe down on University. I'll see.'

'All right. Take your cell phone. Call me if you . . . if you . . . just call me, please.'

'I will. I promise.' He started for the

side door that would lead to the garage.

'Please,' she said, 'one more thing . . . don't take the Lexus. It's such a target. You'll get in trouble. Take the hybrid. Nobody sees them, there are so many around here.'

He sighed, stopped at the credenza near the inside garage door, and switched the sets of keys.

'Wear your warm coat. A night like this, it's nasty out.'

'I'll be in the car.'

'But if you see anything, you might have to get out of the car. Wear your warm coat. Please . . . '

He slid down out of the hills and headed toward MacArthur. The row of motels there were notorious places for hookers to congregate. Johns knew it. They would cruise and eyeball the talent and make a choice. The cheapskates would get service right in their cars. The carriage trade would pull into a motel parking lot and pay for a room as well as for the girl.

Or boy.

11

Was it possible?

Joseph Horton had cruised down Broadway Terrace from Berkeley to Oakland, continued on Broadway and turned right, away from the big Kaiser Hospital on MacArthur. He rolled past the row of motels opposite the darkened Mosswood Park. One hot-sheet joint after another. The Prius wasn't the only car moving slowly past the motels.

At least the previous night's storm had passed over the Bay Area to drop what remained of its moisture as it rose into the Sierras in the Tahoe Basin and down a few hundred feet into the high desert country of western Nevada. If the storm had lingered, there would have been no parade along MacArthur and no point in Joseph's mission. He might as well have stayed home with Carolyn and endured her nightly bouts of grief and rage, as if what had happened was his fault.

The working girls and their pimps were parading on the broad sidewalk in front of the motels. There were enough streetlamps to let them show off their wares, their uniforms of short skirts and high-heel boots, swinging their hips, strutting their stuff in competition for the customers' eyes.

At Manila Avenue Joseph Horton swung right, through a neighborhood of paint and body shops, tire stores, automotive garages as dark at night as the park and probably as dangerous. Right again on Thirty-Eighth Street and back to Broadway. Past a couple of restaurants and bars, then right again on MacArthur.

Was it possible? Among the whores and pimps parading in front of the motels he recognized a familiar figure. Small and painfully thin, she barely resembled the happy, energetic daughter that he and Carolyn had raised. But —

She couldn't possibly match the flashy hookers in their vinyl boots and short skirts, a few of them sporting skin-tight spandex outfits instead, looking like down-on-their-luck superheroines trying to raise capital to use in their endless struggle against the forces of evil.

But there she was. He was almost sure.

The traffic flow was heavy and every foot of curb space was occupied. He pulled into the first motel parking lot he could reach. It was the Uncle Sam. A huge neon figure in red, white, and blue stars and stripes tipped his high hat to passers by. A bright pink sign in the office window flashed 'vacancy.'

He slammed on the brakes and jumped out of the Prius. Then he ran out of the parking lot, back to the sidewalk.

Women of every shade and description used the space as if they were fashion models and the sidewalk was their runway.

And there she was. The red hair. The slim body. The little-girl, just-growing-up hips. How could she . . . How could anyone . . .

She had her back to him. She hadn't seen him. He couldn't run as well as he had twenty or thirty years ago; the decades had cut into his wind as well. He called out, 'Rebi, Rebi, stop! Stop, Rebi!

It's your father, Rebi! Come home, please! Stop! At least talk.'

He felt a heavy impact on the back of his head, and as he tumbled forward, throwing out his hands to break his fall, he thought he might have felt a sharp pain in his back, but there was no certainty at that point. There was a second impact as he hit the sidewalk face down, and everything turned to blackness.

★　★　★

He woke up in bed in a bright room. There were sensors stuck to his chest, and a tube in his arm — he followed it carefully with his eyes — rose to an IV bag hung from a tall hook. Some kind of electronic gadget stood near his bed, numbers flashing and changing in neon blue, and a round CRT with a jagged line moving across its face. Just like hospital shows on TV.

There were one, two, three people in the room with him. One was a heavyset, brown-skinned woman wearing hospital scrubs. There was a male in midnight blue, a silver badge on his uniform chest. Cop. Cop. OPD cop. Right. The third person was a woman wearing a tweed jacket and what looked like a button-down shirt. The last he'd known he was in Oakland, outside that motel, the Uncle Sam Motel, opposite the big park.

And he'd found Rebi. Or thought he'd found her. He was running after her, out of breath, stumbling, and she was running away. Or had she turned at the last moment? Had she turned, and had he seen her face, and had she seen his, had she recognized him? Had she started back? Had she moved toward him instead of away? Had he clasped her in his arms? Had he lifted her in the air the way he had when she was a happy toddler, crowing with love and delight? Had they started for the Prius, started for home?

No, he told himself, that was only a dream.

There had been the impact on the back of his head, the pain in his side, the second impact as he hit the sidewalk. He tried to sit up but he couldn't move in bed. There was a pain in his lower back, at once sharp and hot and intense, and yet remote and fuzzy. His very thoughts were fuzzy. Probably — he was aware enough to figure it out — probably the result of a painkiller. That's what they gave you in hospitals.

The woman in civilian garb was talking to him. She'd been talking for a while, he realized, but he had no idea what she'd been saying. He opened his mouth to reply but nothing came out except a dry gagging sound.

The brown-skinned woman in the hospital scrubs held a glass for him, a glass with a straw, one of those awful glass straws. He didn't know that they used them anymore. He drew on it and felt a wave of freshness in his mouth. The woman took the glass away.

The woman in the tweed jacket said, 'Maybe I'd better start again, do you think, Mr. Horton? You *are* Mr. Horton?'

He managed a small nod. 'I — I am.'

'Mr. Horton, you're a very lucky man.'

'I don't . . . ' Pause, deep breath, try again. 'I don't feel lucky. What happened?'

'You've been hit on the head and stabbed in the back. You're lucky to be alive. Do you know where you are?'

He tried to twist his head around but gave up after one roaring pain. 'Looks like a hospital room,' he managed.

'That's right. You're in Kaiser Permanente Oakland. Do you know how you got here?'

'No — no idea.'

'Officer Torrance — ' The cop nodded to Horton. ' — found you on the sidewalk in front of the Uncle Sam Motel. We're just up the street from there. Kaiser gets a lot of input from that motel row.'

'Got your ID from your wallet, Mr. Horton,' Officer Torrence said. 'It's in the hospital office safe now, with your wristwatch and rings.' He came closer to Joseph's bed. 'Mr. Horton, I very nearly arrested you for soliciting sex with a minor. That's a very serious charge. That's why Ms. Vance is here right now.' He gestured toward the tweed-jacketed woman. 'Ms. Teresa Vance is a deputy prosecutor with the Alameda County District Attorney's office.'

The woman nodded to Joseph. She took over the conversation. 'We're working constantly to suppress the sex trade but it's like playing Whack-A-Mole. We close them down on one street and they move to another. And of course street prostitution is just one facet of the problem. But, Mr. Horton, preying on children — I have to be honest with you, sir. If I had my way, I would throw the book at you. I really would.' She exhaled angrily. 'But the young lady got away in the melee that followed the attack on you. So did your attacker. Probably her pimp. So we'd have a hard time proving this on you, for all that I would like to try. And I hope you've learned your lesson, sir. You came within an inch of your life. I mean that literally. Dr. Chen says that the person who wielded the knife on you was either extremely skillful or you were extremely lucky. As it is, you'll spend some time in this hospital and you'll go home with a scar. But I don't imagine you'll be showing it off at your health club and telling the story of how you got it.'

'But, I — ' Joseph Horton shook his head, or tried to. It hurt too much to do more than move it a fraction of an inch either way. 'I'm no — no child molester.'

'Then what are you? What were you doing out there?'

'I — that girl — '

The tweed-jacketed woman nodded encouragement.

'She's my daughter. I've been looking for her for months. *Months!* My wife keeps saying she must have run away, that she's probably on the Hollywood strip by now, or in New York.'

'Are you serious? Is there a missing persons report on file?'

'Sure. Sure. Filed it months ago. Nobody cares. There are so many of them. Runaways, drug users, diseased, abused. She was only . . . such a pretty thing . . . When she was a little girl we used to play, and . . . ' Joseph Horton fell silent, tears running down his cheeks, too weak or wounded or exhausted to wipe them away. Or too lost in despair.

★   ★   ★

Rigoberto Chocron was a man of his word, give him that. And he insisted that Marvia Plum live up to hers. A full Sunday breakfast at Los Arcos de Oro before they headed for the Route 880 Flea Market.

Rigoberto leaned back, patted his belly and told Marvia Plum, 'Very nice, very nice. Thank you. Now pay the lady.'

Marvia did, and they proceeded to the flea market in her souped-up Falcon. She drove slowly, not letting on that the car was anything other than a forty-year-old beater. Her ID got them into a reserved parking area and VIP entry to the market itself. A huge outdoor motion-picture screen, now tattered with weather and neglect, loomed over the scores of sellers.

A manager offered to guide Marvia and Rigoberto through the lot, but Marvia declined. Rigoberto had assured her that he could find the Space Cadets and she preferred to keep officialdom at arm's length, at least for now.

And it wasn't hard finding the Space Cadets. Yes, there were two of them, an amazing matched set, male and female, both seriously overweight, clad in matching baseball caps and badly faded T-shirts that showed the faint remnants of scenes in outer space. The male Cadet wore his gray ponytail pulled through the strap on the back of his cap. The female Cadet sported Princess Leia side-braids.

They sat beneath a banner blazoned 'Starship Galaxy Enterprises.' Their table was covered with merchandise aimed at the hopeless science fiction devotee: baseball caps harking back to every sci-fi movie or TV extravaganza from *Captain Video* and *Rocky Jones* onward, T-shirts, plastic models, ray guns, DVDs, and super-high-tech electronic gear whose purpose Marvia could only guess at. There were rows of paperbacks with aliens and rocket ships on the covers, pulp magazines and comic books. And one laptop computer. The computer was open, an ever-changing scene of space-ships and alien planets swirling across the monitor.

The male Space Cadet grinned broadly at Marvia and Chocron. Both Space Cadets held up their right hands in a gesture that might have been either a Hebrew blessing or a Vulkanian welcome sign.

The two cadets chanted in perfect harmony. 'Greetings, travelers to alien worlds. In what may we interest you this lovely terra-day?'

Marvia showed her ID. The Cadets came back to earth. 'I'm Lieutenant Plum, Berkeley Police Department.'

'We're in Oakland,' the female Cadet growled.

'Doesn't matter. If you want to make a phone call before you speak with me, feel free.'

The two Cadets exchanged glances. The male spoke up. 'No. Look, ask away. We're honest businesspeople here, just trying to keep the public happy and make an honest space-doubloon or two.'

'Do you recognize this man?' Marvia gestured at Chocron, who shuffled his feet like an embarrassed schoolboy.

The Cadet frowned at Chocron. 'Can't say as I do.' He turned to his partner. 'You recognize this earthling, Plutonia?'

The female Cadet tilted her head and

shot a studious glance at Chocron. 'Can't say as I do, Telesto. Mayhap he was using a shape-changing paradigm and appeared to us as a Martian sand-tiger or a gray.'

'All right.' Marvia rapped her knuckles on the table. 'We're here on business. Did you or did you not sell a laptop computer to this man?'

'Cool your jets, commissioner,' said Plutonia. 'Maybe we did, maybe we didn't. I don't recognize your friend here. When did this alleged sale take place?'

Chocron said, 'Beginning of last semester. I needed it for my course at Laney. That would be September, maybe end of August.'

'Are you certain these are the people who sold you the laptop?'

'Absolutely. Could I forget these two?'

Marvia gave the Space Cadets her tough-cop, this-is-serious-business look. 'Mr. Chocron is certain that he bought the computer from you.'

Plutonia growled, 'Okay, so we sold him the computer. So what? We get some serious merchandise from time to time. Most of our business is *tchotchkes*, but once in a while we'll pick up a nice iPhone or BlackBerry or laptop, and turn it for a little profit. Nothing illegal about that, is there?'

'Not if it's legitimate merchandise.'

'That's all we handle. Rules of the market, if nothing else.'

'Do you keep records? Sales slips, transaction books, anything like that?'

Telesto pointed to the laptop on the table. 'This one isn't for sale. It's the one we run our business out of.'

'All right. Can you look up the transaction with Mr. Chocron? I don't imagine you sell many computers.' Marvia noticed that the computer was literally padlocked to the table.

'No, we don't,' the Cadet conceded. 'Let me see what I can come up with.'

A couple of interested browsers had stopped at the table and Plutonia was pitching them an authentic, studio-certified script for an unproduced *Legion of Space* feature film. The browsers also came in a matched set, male and female, decked out in futuristic regalia, but each of them about a hundred pounds lighter than the Space Cadets.

'Last year?' the male Cadet asked.

'Yes.'

'September twelve. Here it is.' He swung the laptop around. It showed a sales line for one laptop computer, forty-nine dollars plus tax. 'We have a resale license; you know the state inspectors are really tight-assed about collecting sales tax. Pardon my language.'

'Quite a bargain. What did you pay for that, if you could sell it for forty-nine dollars and still make a profit?'

Plutonia turned her attention back from the browsers to Marvia. 'We spend a lot of time at garage sales, thrift stores, close-outs. Even recycling depots. You'd be surprised, Captain; people dump perfectly good equipment.'

'Lieutenant, and thank you.' To the male Cadet, she said, 'Does your record show the customer's identity?'

Cadet Telesto clicked a couple of keys. 'Here it is. Customer's name, John Smith. Means of payment, cash.'

Marvia turned to Chocron. 'Are you John Smith, too?'

'I guess I didn't show much imagination.'

'Never mind. That was you? You didn't get your laptop from somebody else?'

'No.' He shook his head. 'I couldn't forget these dudes, could I? I got it from these Cadets, that's for certain.'

Marvia said, 'All right. This is good. We're getting somewhere. Now, Mister — Telesto?'

'That's right.'

'Let me see your resale license.'

He produced it.

'Mister . . . Watkins. Mr. and Mrs. Watkins. Oscar and Mandy. I take it you're Oscar, then.'

'That's right.'

'Mr. Watkins, this looks pretty clean so far. I take it you didn't insist on seeing ID from John Smith here, but I don't suppose you needed to for a cash transaction. What I need to know is, where did you get the computer? At a yard sale?'

'I'm not sure. So much comes through here.'

'You'd better remember. Try hard.'

Telesto stared into his computer,

clicked a few keys, stared some more. 'Here it is. But I don't know how much good it can do you.'

'Let me worry about it. Speak up now!'

'I got it from a couple of teenagers.'

While Marvia interrogated Oscar Watkins a.k.a Space Cadet Telesto, the browsers had bought the unproduced movie script, a couple of stills, and his-and-hers T-shirts featuring Arnold Schwarzenegger as a killer android from Space Cadet Plutonia. They strolled away hand-in-hand, looking like happy children. Maybe that's what they were.

Mandy Watkins a.k.a. Space Cadet Plutonia had put their money in a cash box. She turned to her partner. 'You through with the computer, Telesto? I need to enter this sale.'

Telesto looked questioningly at Marvia, received an approving nod, and turned the computer over to his partner. 'I found it,' Telesto told Marvia. 'You'll get a laugh out of this. I sold that computer to John Smith here, and I bought it from John Smith. Must be two guys with the same name, right?'

'Did you ask the first Mr. Smith for proof of identity? Proof of ownership of the computer?'

'Captain, ma'am, let's get real. This is a cash-and-carry business. We don't ask our customers to prove who they are. We don't ask our vendors to prove who they are. We buy the merchandise, we mark it up just enough to cover expenses and grocery money, we sell it. We don't look like rich people, do we?'

Marvia suppressed a sigh. Beside her, Chocron was showing signs of restlessness. 'Just a few more minutes, Rigoberto, and we'll get out of here,' she said.

'I'm hungry, Lieutenant.'

'I'll buy lunch.'

That seemed to mollify him.

'All right, Mr. and Mrs. Watkins. I want you both to concentrate. You bought the computer from a man named John Smith. He had a female companion. What was her name?'

Space Cadet Plutonia said, 'Mary Smith.'

Oh, great. 'No ID?'

Negative headshake.

'How about a description?'

Telesto spoke first. 'The guy had dirty blond hair. Bad complexion. About five, oh, five eight or nine. Slim build. Kind of dirty and sickly-looking. Might have weighed a hundred forty pounds, max. I'd say he was sixteen. Maybe a little older, not much.'

'Any scars, birthmarks? No? You say his hair was dirty blond. White male, what color eyes?'

'I couldn't tell. He looked away a lot, didn't want to make eye contact.'

'Could you tell if he was right- or left-handed?'

'He was left-handed,' Plutonia put in. 'I remember. He wanted to show us that the computer worked. He used his left hand on the touchpad.'

'See?' Telesto said. 'She knows everything!' He reached over and patted Plutonia's hand. Love will always find a way.

'What about his companion?'

Plutonia said, 'I was really sad for her. She was a little thing; she'd blow away in a strong breeze. And she could have been so pretty. Couldn't have been more than thirteen years old. I could hardly tell what color her hair was, it looked so dirty, but it must have been red. Not just auburn. Not one of those bright red wig colors they wear nowadays, either. Real, classic Titian red. I'd love to have hair that color. And green eyes, beautiful deep green eyes, and skin . . . She looked so dirty and sickly, but if she'd just let somebody take her in hand and clean her up and feed her up, oh, you'd fall in love with her in a minute. Anybody would.'

Marvia asked if the Space Cadets had a record of what they'd paid the Smiths for the computer, and if the Smiths had given any indication of where or how they had come into possession of it.

A little more clicking and Oscar Watkins said, 'We paid them thirty dollars for it. I remember we tried it out before we'd pay anything; that was when the kid wanted to give us a demo. The thing worked fine. Case looked a little battered, but the screen lit up and there was even software loaded in it. Worked fine.'

'Do you remember anything about the

files on the computer?'

Oscar Watkins shook his head. 'Sorry. The operating system ran. I opened a text file and typed in a few sentences just to see if it worked and it did. That was all.'

'And where they got the computer?'

'Said somebody had left it in front of a house with a 'Free' sign on it. Must have been moving. The kids said they left a bookcase and an easy chair and a couch, but all they took was the computer.'

'Did they say where that happened?'

'Nope. We didn't ask. They didn't tell.'

Telesto and Plutonia had no address for John Smith and Mary Smith. No ID. Nothing. Two sickly-looking teenagers. A computer that came and went. Now what?

Chocron said, 'I'm pretty hungry.'

This time Marvia did sigh. 'All right.' She left two cards, one for Plutonia and one for Telesto. She suppressed another sigh. 'You know the drill. If either of these kids shows up again, or if you remember anything, give me a call. Even if you think it's unimportant, you can never tell. And thank you very much for your help.'

As Marvia and Rigoberto walked away, an excited six-year-old wearing a superhero cape was dragging his so-respectable-looking parents to the Starship Galaxy Enterprises sales table, and Space Cadets Plutonia and Telesto were warming up their welcoming smiles and interplanetary greeting gestures. Or maybe Hebrew blessings.

Chocron said, 'Is it lunch time?'

'Pick your place. And then we can head back to the office and start that paperwork going.'

'You a woman of your word, Lieutenant.'

'My great pride, Mister Chocron, my great pride.'

12

Carolyn Horton was furious. 'Look at you! Tubes coming out of you everyplace! Two black eyes! How did you manage that? You said you never even saw him, so how did you get those shiners? Bandages on your head like some kind of hoodlum. I warned you. I said don't go, or if you have to go, take me along. But you had to run out and be the big hero.'

'I asked if you wanted to come along.'

'Oh, all right, so you did. I wasn't feeling good. There's no use. You don't know where she is. She's probably in Hollywood putting out for every pervert who comes along with a five-dollar bill in his hand.'

'I don't think so.'

'Well, I do. And so does that detective we hired, what's his name — '

'Kellen Jamison.'

'Whatever his name is, that slickster. So he took our money to tell us she wasn't in

Berkeley anymore. Probably in L.A. We could have figured that out for ourselves.'

'I still don't believe it, Carolyn. I know our girl. She wouldn't stray that far from home.'

'Then somebody took her. Took a helpless child, probably drugged her, threw her in the back of a car, next thing you know they could be anyplace. Anyplace. You've heard those stories about Argentina. And you had to be a hero and go playing at private eye, and look at you, look at you. I had everything, and now I don't have Rebi. And look at you, look how close I came to losing you too. Picking a fight with some brute, some pimp, what did you expect?'

'Please, Carolyn. I'm in pain. Please let up.'

'How can I let up when you're acting like a fool, trying to look like a hero?'

'I saw her, Carolyn. I almost touched her. I saw her and I started after her, I called her name. 'Rebi,' I said, 'Rebi, wait, Rebi, come back, it's Daddy,' and she turned around. She turned around,

Carolyn. I saw her face. It was our Rebi. I'm sure of it.'

'And you told the police? They still think you're a pervert, a child molester who just crossed the wrong people. And look what it got you, Joey. Look at yourself.'

That brought a trace of a smile. 'I can't do that. I don't have a mirror and I can't get to the bathroom.'

'Well, just as well. You're a sight. I'd be ashamed to be seen with you.'

'Okay, Carolyn, okay, you won't have to. Not for a while. Dr. Chen says I'm going to be here for a while.'

Carolyn stood up and poured herself a glass of water from the carafe near Joseph's bed. She stood at the window and looked out onto MacArthur Boulevard. 'It looks so innocent, so ordinary in the daytime. And at night, a street of shame. A street of shame.'

'Very dramatic. Those are just motels in the next block.'

'Full of whores and pimps and the perverts who patronize them.'

Joseph said, 'I saw her, Carolyn. Nothing can convince me otherwise. Rebi is still nearby, and there's still a chance we can rescue her from . . . from what happened to her.'

'And if we do? She'll just go back to them. They've destroyed her, those perverts, monsters, criminals. She's ruined now. What can we do, keep her prisoner? Lock her up like an animal? She'll gnaw through her chains and go back to them.' She drank some more water. 'Did you tell them about her? Did you tell them that she was our daughter, not some cheap streetwalker?'

'I told them.'

'And did they believe you?'

'I told that district attorney, Teresa Vance. I told her everything.'

'About the missing person report? About juvenile hall?'

'I told you, Carolyn, I told her everything. There's nothing to keep secret. Not now. Besides, everything is on record. She would have found out anyway.'

'And what are they doing? Treating you like a criminal for trying to rescue your own flesh and blood from those bloodsuckers, those human vampires who use innocent children to make money off perverts every night?'

'Please, Carolyn. Please.' His face was twisted with pain. 'I can't take any more. Not now. I have to rest.'

She poured some water and held the glass for him. 'Here, drink. You need the straw? No? Good, just drink.' She put the glass back on the tray. 'I'm going home. I'll come back later.'

'Please, yes.'

She stamped out of the room. The door closed softly behind her. She made her way to a visitors' lounge and sat down and wept.

★ ★ ★

Driving from downtown Berkeley to Grand Lake in Oakland took a while thanks to freeway traffic. Officer Jo Rossi and Hobart Lindsey used the time to plan their inquiry. Rossi was interested in the laptop as stolen property and conceivably as a murder weapon. Lindsey's interest was in the Wallace Thompson file on the hard drive. If it was still there. Rossi suggested that Lindsey go first. The uniform and badge and gun lurking behind him would give some impetus to his questions, but the presence of Lindsey as a civilian would make the pair less threatening. At least that was their strategy.

Universal Data Services, Inc. was located on Grand Avenue a few storefronts up the block from the refurbished Grand Lake Theater. A donut shop on one side, a Laundromat on the other. A display window full of computers and other equipment. Busy little gnomes in the back of the store, visible from the street, doing their magic tricks on gray boxes and glowing monitor screens.

Berkeley Officer Jo Rossi pulled the black-and-white into a convenient parking place. A slim young man sitting behind a desk put down a cell phone and advanced to the counter to greet Lindsey and Jo Rossi. Lindsey was stunned. '*Hakeem?*'

The young man said, 'Yes. Do I know you, sir?'

'Hakeem White?'

'That's right.'

'I'm Hobart Lindsey, International

Surety. This is Officer Rossi, Berkeley Police Department.'

'Of course. Lieutenant Plum's friend. Jamie Wilkerson's mom.'

'Marvia told me about your father's death, Hakeem. I'm very sorry. It must be very hard for you.'

'Thank you. We've got a woman who comes in while I'm away from home. She does a good job. But I'm afraid I've neglected my old friends since I moved back from Seattle.' He paused. 'But what can I do for you, sir?'

'I'm looking for a laptop computer.'

White laughed. 'You've come to the right place. We're mainly a service and repair company, but we sell the things, too. New or used. Or we'll build one for you — just tell Max what you want and we'll pull it together for you.'

Lindsey asked, 'Who's Max?'

White jerked a thumb toward the elves' workshop. 'Max is our hardware maven. Anything you want, he'll build it for you. He could build a super-processor out of a broken transistor radio and a couple of flashlights. He's our Hannibal Lecter. And our software genius is Fabia Rabinowitz. She was making more money at UC, but she couldn't stand the bureaucracy so we got her. Lucky us!'

Lindsey couldn't help asking what Hakeem White did.

'I'm the running-dog capitalist exploiter. I sit on my posterior all day counting my profits while the workers suffer.' He paused. 'But seriously, you want a laptop, happy to accommodate. Why do you need a police escort, though?'

Jo Rossi stepped into the conversation. 'I don't think you quite understand why we're here, sir. Mr. Lindsey isn't looking for just any laptop computer. He's looking for a particular one. And I'm looking for it, as well. For quite different reasons.'

'Can you describe the machine?'

Jo Rossi checked her notebook and read off the manufacturer, model number, even the machine's serial number.

Hakeem White frowned. 'And what makes you think we have it?'

Lindsey said, 'I've been tracing this machine from owner to owner, Hakeem. It seems to get traded every few days. The last owner I've been able to locate is a Miss Jade Montoya.' He was careful to give the words their Spanish pronunciation. 'Music student at Cal. She told me that the machine quit working on her. Your service was recommended and she brought it in to be repaired.'

White nodded thoughtfully. 'Okay. And then what?'

'She told me that you gave her an estimate and she decided it wasn't worth the expense of having it fixed.'

White nodded. 'That happens. The technology changes so fast, by the time you get an old machine up and running again, sometimes you might as well just recycle it and buy a new one.'

He turned away and pulled open the top drawer of a four-drawer filing cabinet. Extracted a manila folder. Laid it on the counter between himself and Lindsey and Jo Rossi. 'We still use the old ways for some things,' he laughed. Then, 'Here it is. Exactly as you described it. Motherboard was shot. Parts and labor on that, yeah, would hardly have been worth the trouble.'

'So — where is it now?' Lindsey asked. 'Did you just throw it out, or salvage it for parts?'

'Neither.' He stepped away from the counter, weaving through desks and benches to get to the gnomes' workshop. Lindsey heard him say, 'Max, can you get away from that for a minute? Got a couple of people here you need to talk to.'

White returned, accompanied by an Asian male in his thirties clad in a white lab coat. 'Max, Hobart Lindsey, old-time friend of Jamie Wilkerson's mom. And Officer, uh, Rossi, right?'

'Right.'

'Mr. Lindsey, Officer Rossi, this is Max Chen, star manipulator of all things molecular and electronic. He can tell you about that laptop.'

'Why is that?' Lindsey said.

'Because I gave it to him. Seemed a shame to toss it. Didn't think we could sell it, not for enough dollars to get back our costs.'

Jo Rossi said, 'Is this true, Mr. Chen?'

Chen nodded. 'That's right.'

'And you have the computer now?'

''Fraid not.'

'All right, sir. I hope you're not being difficult. This is a very serious matter. I ask you, what did you do with the computer?'

'I got Fabia to load it up with a lot of games and gave it to my sister's kids to play with.'

Lindsey and Rossi exchanged glances. 'Your sister's kids,' Rossi echoed.

'That's right. They love to play computer games. I put in a wi-fi card, Fabia loaded the software, and they're off to the land of knights and ladies and dragons. That's one day. Next, they're on another planet. Or flying around shooting superhero rays at atomic monsters. Or saving the world from the next pandemic. Their mom wants them to use the thing for their schoolwork, but what are you going to do with a pair of eight-year-old twins?'

Lindsey and Rossi had their notebooks out and pens in hand. The cop was faster on the verbal draw. 'I need to know your sister's full name and contact information.'

Max Chen smiled. 'She's right nearby.

Dr. Claudia Chen. She works at the Knife and Gun Club.'

'The what?'

'Kaiser Hospital. Down on MacArthur. You can get there in ten minutes unless it's rush hour.'

'And this club?' Lindsey asked.

'That's what they call the ER down there. Especially docs who pull weekend and night duty. The Knife and Gun Club.' He gave them a cell-phone number.

Jo Rossi asked, 'What are the children's names?'

'William and Hillary.'

'You've got to be kidding.'

'Nope. Kids take a lot of ribbing at school, but those are their names. They're twins, though, and they stick together. Must be nice to know that somebody has your back all the time.'

Jo Rossi asked Max Chen if his sister would be on duty now. He didn't know for sure but he thought so. Rossi tried the cell-phone number and got voice mail. She left her message, requested a call back, and told Claudia Chen that she was on her way to Kaiser right now.

Claudia Chen was baffled. Why did the Berkeley Police Department want to know about her kids' computer games, and what was this insurance investigator doing, poking his nose into the matter?

But the police officer explained that the computer was stolen property. It was evidence in a potential felony trial. 'Where is the computer now, please?' Rossi had her pencil poised over her notebook.

Claudia Chen raised her eyes to an oversized wall clock. 'They'd still be at school. Billy and Hilly. They probably have it with them.'

'I'll need directions to the school. And your home address, too, Dr. Chen. Just for the record.'

Claudia Chen provided the information. 'Benjamin Bannacker Elementary School, Room 7B,' she concluded, 'Ms. Templeton.'

Back to the black-and-white.

The school was located in the hills above Piedmont Avenue, an older, affluent section of Oakland. No gang activity here; commercial security service stickers in street-facing windows. After dark private patrol cruisers whispered by in the darkness, you could be sure of that.

When a uniformed police officer appeared in the doorway of Ms. Templeton's classroom, a buzz ran through the seated students. The teacher was a trim, dark-skinned, gray-haired woman, the kind who terrified children the first day of each school year and with whom they fell in love before a month was out.

She signaled to the students and they dutifully opened books and began studying, or at least pretended to begin studying, while their teacher conferred with the visitors. After a brief conference Ms. Templeton re-entered the classroom and summoned a boy and girl to join her in the hallway.

'William, Hillary, this is Officer Rossi and Mr. Lindsey. They need to take your computer.'

William started to protest but Hillary asked more calmly, 'Why?'

Ms. Templeton explained that the computer was needed as part of a police investigation.

Hillary nodded understandingly. William exclaimed, 'Cool!' He ran back into the classroom and returned with the computer. Officer Rossi took it from his hands.

Hillary asked, 'Will we get it back?'

Jo Rossi said, 'I'm really not sure. It's evidence.'

'But our Uncle Max gave it to us,' William whined.

'I'm sorry. I'm sure he'll get you another.'

Jo Rossi gave the twins a receipt for their computer and handed a copy to Ms. Templeton. Then they headed back to Grand Avenue.

* * *

'Sure, we can clone the disk,' said Hakeem White. 'No problem. But then what will you do with it? You want it on an external hard drive, or what?'

Lindsey said that would be great. He'd left his own machine back at the Woodfin. Once he got back there he could slip the new drive into a USB port and either use the new drive as his data source or transfer the crucial file to the computer itself. If he had that file!

Jo Rossi could have the original, the machine stolen from Gordon Simmons, the machine that had been used as an impromptu weapon, the weapon that sent Simmons crashing backward into the brick structure and brought bone splinters slamming into his brain. Hobart Lindsey would settle happily for the clone.

White said, 'Come on then, this will only take a little while. Max and Fabia will get the thing set up for you. We'll go next door for a cup of coffee and a donut.'

Jo Rossi took the time to call her office at BPD. When she got off the phone they settled in for a dose of sugar and caffeine. Then it was Lindsey's turn.

Marvia Plum's voice came through the cell phone. 'Rossi says you've got it.'

Lindsey admitted that was the case.

'That file you wanted on it?'

'I don't know yet. I will in a little while.'

'Okay. Good luck. Listen, Bart, we're having a little get-together at my house tonight. You're invited. You'll be at the

Woodfin? Good. Lobby around seven-thirty, okay?'

That was definitely okay.

13

The new drive booted up, and Lindsey found Gordon Simmons's Tony Clydesdale novels neatly lined up in a directory titled *Wallace Thompson*. Each novel was in a folder, annotated with the date Simmons had started work, character and setting notes, plot outline, date of completion and date of publication. The last folder in the directory was titled *The Ruby Red Pup*.

The Ruby Red Pup.

And Rigoberto Chocron's — Steve Damon's — one and only thriller was *The Emerald Cat*. At least Chocron had been honest when he admitted that he didn't have much imagination. Lindsey opened his copy of *The Emerald Cat* and laid it on the writing desk in his hotel room beside his newly enhanced laptop computer. He riffled the pages to the novel's opening scene.

Troy Percheron pushed his battered fedora onto the back of his head as he climbed onto the barstool and leaned wearily against the mahogany. He knew that the name of the establishment was spelled out in the glass window behind him. Looking straight ahead into the back-bar mirror, the reversed lettering got the turnaround treatment again so he was able to read it. Spelled out in lurid green neon it read, 'The Emerald Cat.' An image of a stylized feline completed the display.

Percheron felt a hand on his wrist. He looked down. The fingers were long and thin, the nails polished an astonishing shade of green, almost as if the color had been chosen to match the neon reflecting from the back-bar mirror.

'Buy a girl a drink, sailor?' The woman breathed sexuality. Her green satin blouse was cut low, showing a pair of gorgeous headlights that could have caught the attention of a blind paraplegic.

'Why, if it isn't my old sweetheart Helena Cairo. How are things in the nasty business, Helena?'

The green-jacketed bartender cleared his throat, getting Troy's attention. 'The usual, Troy?' he rasped. A brass badge on his jacket read 'Marty.' He was one of those bozos who insisted on wearing a ponytail even though he was bald on top and gray in back.

Percheron nodded. 'And give the lady anything she wants.'

Not exactly great literature, but certainly as good as several hundreds of others published every year.

Lindsey turned his attention to his computer screen, to the opening of *The Ruby Red Pup*.

Tony Clydesdale pushed his battered fedora onto the back of his head as he climbed onto the barstool and leaned wearily against the mahogany. He knew that the name of establishment was spelled out in the glass window behind him. Looking straight ahead into the back-bar mirror, the reversed lettering got the turnaround treatment again so he was able to read it. Spelled out in lurid blood-red neon, it read, 'The Ruby Red Pup.' An image of a stylized canine completed the display.

Clydesdale felt a hand on his wrist. He looked down. The fingers were long and thin, the nails polished an astonishing shade of crimson, almost as if the color had been chosen to match the neon reflecting from the back-bar mirror.

'Buy a girl a drink, sailor?' The woman breathed sexuality. Her scarlet satin blouse was cut low, showing a pair of gorgeous headlights that could have caught the attention of a blind paraplegic.

'Why, if it isn't my old sweetheart Selena Thebes. How are things in the nasty business, Selena?'

The crimson-jacketed bartender cleared his throat, getting Tony's attention. 'The usual, Tony?' he rasped. A brass badge on his jacket read 'Morty.' He was one of those bozos who insisted on wearing a ponytail even though he was bald on top and gray in back.

Clydesdale nodded. 'And give the lady anything she wants.'

Lindsey decided to give it another try. He flipped the pages to a chapter break and read the first lines of Chapter Twelve:

Percheron winced as the bucket of ice water sloshed across his battered face. Elmer hadn't removed the ice cubes, either, and they slammed into Percheron's wounded features, almost eliciting a groan of pain, but Percheron wouldn't give Elmer that satisfaction. The monstrous moron grinned happily, bloody drool sliding between the jagged stumps of the teeth that Percheron's fists had slugged away during their free-for-all.

Lindsey did a word search on 'bucket of ice water.' The monitor screen blinked once, and up popped the matching phrase and the surrounding paragraph:

Clydesdale winced as the bucket of ice water sloshed across his battered face. Homer hadn't removed the ice cubes, either, and they slammed into Clydesdale's wounded features, almost eliciting a groan of pain, but Clydesdale wouldn't give

Homer that satisfaction. The monstrous moron grinned happily, bloody drool sliding between the jagged stumps of the teeth that Clydesdale's fists had slugged away during their free-for-all.

One more, one more. Not that he needed any more convincing than what he'd had, but one more anyway, just for good measure. He flipped to the last page of the paperback novel and read:

Toeing the remains of what was left of Elmer after his fourteen-floor tumble from the roof of the Union Jack Hotel, Helena Cairo pressed her voluptuous body hard against the muscular form of Troy Percheron.

'We can have some fun if you want to, baby,' Percheron growled. 'But if you think that's gonna keep your pretty little hindquarters out of the big ladies' lockup in the valley, you've got another think coming.'

Gordon Simmons's file said:

Toeing the remains of what was left of Homer after his fourteen-floor tumble from the roof of the Stars and Stripes Hotel, Selena Thebes pressed her voluptuous body hard against the muscular form of Tony Clydesdale.

'We can have some fun if you want to, baby,' Clydesdale growled. 'But if you think that's gonna keep your pretty little hindquarters out of the big ladies' lockup in the valley, you've got another think coming.'

The case had looked bad for Gordian House — and consequently for International Surety — from the start. But this was the last straw, the smoking gun, the final nail in the coffin, all rolled into one.

Lindsey picked up the phone and punched in the number of Eric Coffman's office on Vine Street. The office manager put him through to Coffman's young associate, Kelly McGee.

'Mr. Lindsey?'

He admitted that he was who he was.

'Mr. Coffman phoned and asked me to give you this message. He's out of

Intensive Care now and in a private room. He'd like to talk with you. You are to come to Alta Bates; come up to his room. They'll direct you at the lobby desk.'

Lindsey thanked the young lawyer and headed from Emeryville, up to the hospital on Ashby Avenue in Berkeley.

When he got to Eric Coffman's room he found Coffman looking better than he'd feared and worse than he'd hoped. Miriam Coffman was there, reading to her husband from a hardcover book. He caught a glimpse of the dust jacket. She was reading *Enemies, A Love Story* by Isaac Bashevis Singer. Rebecca had presumably returned to her charges in Oakland.

Not sure how to announce himself, Lindsey performed the English butler's discreet cough stunt. Eric Coffman had been lying with eyes closed, either sleeping or listening to his wife's rendition of the Singer narrative. Now he opened his eyes and managed a small smile.

Miriam Coffman closed the book and turned. 'Hobart.' He nodded. 'Thank you for coming, Hobart. I know you were here when Eric first came in, but everything was so — was in such a whirl. Did I even say hello? We were expecting you for dinner and . . . it didn't work out.'

The lawyer's head was still bandaged, and the darkness around his eyes made him look more like Raymond Burr than ever. One arm was semi-immobilized, an IV tube providing a steady drip into his vein. 'So, Lindsey, did you bring a camera? I want you to be careful — photograph me only from my good side.'

'And what side is that?' What a relief! If the injured man could joke, that was half the battle right there.

Miriam Coffman said, 'Is this a social visit, or do you two big men want to talk business?'

'Up to your husband,' Lindsey said. 'I'd phoned Eric's office, and what's-her-name — '

Coffman growled, 'McGee. Kelly McGee.'
'Right.'
'She was top of her class at Boalt. You can tell the law students on the Cal

campus — they all dress like Republicans. Smart as a whip. What did she tell you?'

'To hustle over to Alta Bates for a clambake.'

'Good. Miriam, this is going to be business for a little while. Why don't you go home and rest? You've been here for so many hours, I don't want you getting sick taking care of me.' Then, to Lindsey: 'I've been thinking about this case of the M-and-M versus Gordian. Lying here, you know, once the morphine wears off and you get your mind back, there's too much time to think. You see that thing behind you?'

Lindsey turned and saw a television receiver mounted high in a corner of the room.

'They gave me a remote. What you call good service. All of three channels. I have my choice of Oprah, Jerry, and Dr. Phil. Hooray for Hollywood. I have a little trouble, yet, holding a book and reading. God bless my beloved spouse for reading to me. You ever read Isaac Singer? You don't have to be Jewish, you know.'

'Eric, I'm really happy to see you're getting to be yourself again. But was there a business reason for this summons, or did you just want another visitor?'

'Hobart, lying in this bed, I've had hours to stare at the ceiling, stare at the window, stare at those trees and the birds coming and going. So I figure, why not accumulate some billable hours?'

'Doing what?'

'Thinking about Gordian and that fool Jack Burnside. I've had a couple of meetings with Marston and Morse's lawyer, Jenny Caswell. She's a decent sort, not eager to get out the flamethrowers. And her principal, Paula Morse — '

'I've met her.'

'Then you know, she doesn't really want to start hurling grenades either.'

'So we settle, right? Look, Eric, I have to tell you that I've recovered Gordon Simmons's computer. It wound up at a company in Oakland. The motherboard was fried. At least that's what they told me. Whatever that means. Anyway, they got the thing repaired and cloned the hard drive. I have a copy. It has all of

Simmons's Tony Clydesdale novels on it. Including an unpublished one called *The Ruby Red Pup* that is virtually identical to *The Emerald Cat* by Steve Damon.'

Coffman opened his Raymond Burr eyes wider. 'What do you mean, virtually identical?'

'I mean, all Damon did — by the way, his real name is Rigoberto Chocron, lives in Oakland — all he did was change the names and the colors. Tony Clydesdale became Troy Percheron, Selena Thebes became Helena Cairo, the Ruby Red Pup became the Emerald Cat. If Burnside insists on going to court, Jenny Caswell is going to mop the floor with us.'

'Ouch!' Coffman nodded agreement. Lindsey wasn't sure whether the exclamation referred to their legal situation or to the pain the movement caused him. 'So, Lindsey, as I was saying before I was so rudely interrupted — '

'Sorry.'

'It's okay. A couple of concepts we guardians of the public weal like to toss around. Due diligence. Full disclosure. Are you familiar with these? You must be.

In your line of work, you'd have been out the door and looking for another job in five minutes if you didn't know about these things. Have you read the contract between International Surety and Gordian House? Yes? Good. Then you know there's a due diligence clause in it. There has to be.'

'There is.'

'And that means, what?'

'It means the full disclosure by either party in any contractual relationship of any factor which may have a negative effect upon the interests of the other party, O Socratic One.'

'Good. And what does full disclosure mean?'

'As they say in all the courtroom dramas, the truth, the whole truth, and nothing but the truth.'

'Right. Good. Especially the whole truth. Did Steve Damon — you say his real name is Chocron — reveal to Gordian House that he was not the actual author of *The Emerald Cat*? Didn't his contract with Gordian have the usual clause to that effect, and that the property was truly his, unencumbered and his to dispose of? Did our Mister Chocron lie to Jack Burnside?'

'Burnside never met Chocron,' Lindsey said. 'Everything went through Chocron's agent, Rachael Gottlieb.'

'Really?'

'I interviewed her as well. She's a real throwback. Fancy tea, medieval chanting music, embroidered pillows on the floor.'

'Never mind that. If she signed the contract with Gordian, then she and her client, Chocron, share responsibility. But more to the point, I take it that Jack Burnside did not investigate to make sure that the book was what Gottlieb or Chocron or both of them claimed it was. That is, an original work, written by Chocron and unencumbered.'

'And what does that mean to us, Eric?'

'It means that Jack Burnside brought his troubles down on himself. He didn't exercise due diligence; didn't obtain full disclosure from Gottlieb and Chocron. He can go after them if he wants to, if M-and-M sues him and prevails. But from what you tell me, Gottlieb won't have a sou to pay him with. And Chocron — what about him? Any assets?'

'I don't think so. He's a very slippery character. No known address, picks up telephone messages at a little restaurant out in Fruitvale.'

'Okay, okay. Lindsey, my boy, I think we have to have a very serious chat with Jack Burnside of Gordian House. If he is willing to make a reasonable settlement with M-and-M, I will advise International Surety to pay the two dollars. If he insists on fighting their claim, I will advise International Surety to deny his claim. Then he can engage counsel and bring suit against I.S., and if that happens I will happily represent I.S. and give Mr. Burnside a legal bloody nose.'

★   ★   ★

As soon as Lindsey got back to the Woodfin, he sent his report to Denver. He was getting ready for a refreshing shower when his cell phone rang.

Ducky Richelieu.

Richelieu didn't waste any time on

pleasantries. 'Whose side are you on, Lindsey?'

'I guess you've read my report.'

'You bet I have. I sent you out there to look into this thing and save the company some money. And you're recommending that we pay these candy people. Why am I paying you?'

'Candy people? Oh, I get it.'

'Get what?'

It dawned on Lindsey that Richelieu had not made a joke. Not that the man had ever been known for his scintillating wit. He really thought that International Surety was involved with a commercial confectioner.

'No, Mr. Richelieu, M-and-M isn't the candy company. They're Marston and Morse, Publishers. This is a copyright and commercial fraud suit.'

'And you want to throw in the towel before the first round even begins.'

'Mr. Richelieu, our client is in the wrong. If he fights he's going to lose. If that happens we either have to pay up or reject his claim, and then he'll sue us. Everybody loses. As our local counsel advises us, pay the two dollars.'

Visions of Victor Moore and Edward Arnold . . .

Richelieu grumbled into the telephone. Lindsey could see the man, barricaded behind his desk like the last defender of a fallen city, searching desperately for an escape route that he would not find.

'What are you going to do now, Lindsey?'

'I'm going to set up a meeting as soon as I can with our counsel, Eric Coffman, and the other parties. J.P. Caswell for M-and-M. Paula Paige Morse if she'll attend. Our esteemed client, Jack Burnside. And Rachael Gottlieb, the literary agent.'

'What about the author?'

'You mean Rigoberto Chocron? If we need anything more from him we'd do better to try and get a deposition. He's much too slippery a character to show up at a meeting. But it wouldn't hurt to have Mrs. Simmons there. She'll be party to the M-and-M suit if it happens.'

Richelieu growled. 'I don't like it, but anything else I can think of is worse. All right, go ahead. Keep me posted. And, Lindsey, what about the local gendarmerie? Weren't you pretty chummy with a lady cop out there?'

'I was.'

'You were, eh? No more? That go *pfttt*?'

'Not exactly. We're still friends. I've had some cooperation from the police department.'

A long silence. Then: 'All right. Break a leg, comrade.'

⋆   ⋆   ⋆

Lindsey was in the lobby within fifteen minutes. He stood gazing out the huge glass window at a black night punctuated only by streetlamps and the lights of passing vehicles. A storm had roared in off the Gulf of Alaska and the entire west coast, from Vancouver to San Luis Obispo, was taking a soaking. At least, so said the local weather reporters.

Marvia Plum's forty-year-old Ford Falcon rolled to a halt beneath the hotel's marquee. The doorman on duty leaned to open the passenger door, open umbrella in his free hand, a look of palpable disdain on his face.

An attractive African-American woman climbed from the little car. She wore a tan raincoat and matching floppy-brimmed hat.

Puzzled, Lindsey exited the hotel lobby. The woman extended her hand. 'I'm Mary Jones. Marvia's preparing dinner. She asked Tyrone and me to pick you up.'

Lindsey shook her hand. He leaned into the Falcon.

'Tyrone?'

'Mr. Lindsey. How long has it been?'

'Hobart, please. Or just Bart. And — since that crazy affair with the painter's model. Fifteen years, easily. I still remember that Volvo you tarted up for me.'

Tyrone Plum laughed. 'Come on, don't make Mary stand there in the cold and rain. Get in the car.'

As Tyrone piloted the Falcon to the Plum family home on Bonar Street, Mary Jones introduced herself. She and Tyrone were close friends, and she and Marvia were like sisters. She'd heard about

Lindsey countless times. Meeting him was like encountering a character from a novel. All Lindsey could think of to say was that he hoped he wouldn't disappoint her.

The house on Bonar Street had received a coat of paint since Lindsey was last there. Other than that, at least at night, it had not changed visibly. Tyrone pulled the Falcon into the driveway. Lights shone on the porch, and Lindsey thought he heard music coming from inside the house.

They were the last guests to arrive. Hakeem White and another woman were sitting in the living room. They jumped up when Lindsey entered with Tyrone Plum and Mary Jones. Hakeem gave Lindsey a grin. 'Haven't seen you for hours.' Without waiting for a response, he introduced his wife. Masani White, Hakeem announced proudly, was a Luo. He'd met her on a vacation trip to Africa. 'I went home to find my roots and I found my bride.' Masani White glowed.

Opposite them, Lindsey recognized Jamie Wilkerson. He was all grown up, and holding hands with a beautiful woman wearing a turquoise satin blouse and tan trousers.

Wilkerson jumped up. 'Mr. Lindsey! What a treat! You'll have to fill me in on the past dozen years.' He shook Lindsey's hand and helped his companion to her feet. 'You've never met my wife, Tanya. Remember that brat from around the corner? Look at her now!'

Marvia Plum emerged from the kitchen. She crossed the room to Lindsey and gave him a small kiss on the cheek. 'Everyone sit down. Tyrone, lend a hand. Drinks and snacks.' The result was beverages all around, and cheese and crackers and celery stalks on a tray.

Chamber music came from concealed speakers. Lindsey didn't recognize the composition and asked what it was.

'That's a Cole Perkinson quartet,' Mary supplied.

Tyrone said, 'Courtesy of Mary. She wouldn't claim credit, but it's her doing. Great music.'

Lindsey admitted that he'd never heard of Cole Perkinson.

Mary said, 'I actually met him once. He came to KRED.'

'Mary's music director there,' Tyrone supplied.

'He showed up just to introduce himself. A wonderful man. I love his music. I stocked up on it at KRED. I don't know how he heard about us, but he was in town as guest conductor at the Oakland Symphony and he just walked into KRED and asked for the music director. I almost fainted when he thanked me for playing his music. He said he'd been channel-surfing in his rented car and he heard his own music and came over to say hello.' She handed Lindsey a CD jewel box. The pamphlet featured a picture of Perkinson, gray-haired, portly, tuxedoed, wielding a baton. He was back-lit, his very dark skin outlined in a nimbus against a black background. 'He died in 2004. You just wait. There's a renaissance coming.'

Lindsey said, 'I thought . . . I hope you don't mind . . . I've always thought of black, er, African composers as writing jazz or, ah, hop-hip — '

'Hip-hop,' Hakeem White corrected.

'Anyway . . . '

'Don't be embarrassed, most people think that,' Mary said. 'Including most black people. That's my mission in life, to educate everyone about our classical music. Look at this.' She handed him another CD, selected from a row in a bookcase. The cover featured a black man in a powdered wig decked out like an eighteenth-century dandy. Like Cole Perkinson, he was poised as if conducting an orchestra, but instead of a baton he held a fencing foil upraised. 'Bet you never heard of Joseph de Bologne, Mr. Lindsey.'

'Please — Bart.'

'He was a brilliant composer, violinist, harpsichordist. He's my personal hero. Well, after Cole Perkinson. Joseph de Bologne was born on Christmas Day, 1745 on the island of Guadaloupe. He was a great swordsman, too. Fled Guadeloupe after he killed an enemy in a duel. He was personally pardoned by the King of France. A brilliant musician. At the time he was known as *Le Mozart Noir*, but I personally think of Mozart as *Le Bologne Blanc*.

Joseph was eleven when Mozart was born. I'm still researching the matter, but I think Mozart knew Bologne's music and was influenced by it.'

Lindsey shook his head. 'Why haven't I ever heard of this man?'

Mary's expression might be called a smile, but it was not a happy smile. 'Did you know that France had eliminated slavery in all its colonies in the eighteenth century? When the 'great liberator' Napoleon became emperor, he reinstituted slavery in the colonies. In 1803. That's a day that will live in infamy — in my book, anyway. After that, Bologne's music was forgotten. I won't exactly say it was suppressed. Joseph was dead by then; at least he didn't have to see what happened. His music just quietly disappeared.' She paused for breath.

Marvia appeared in the doorway. 'Come on, everyone.'

As she got up, Mary said, 'I'm bringing him back. My mission in life. Joseph de Bologne, and Cole Perkinson, and all the rest.'

Marvia's dining room was well lit. A shelf along one wall was lined with brightly colored porcelain figures, Mammies and Uncle Remuses and others that would have been long since removed from any white household but were historical reminders in this one. The room was decorated with colorful canvases. Again, Lindsey had to plead ignorance until they were identified as the work of Charles Bibbs and Margaret Warfield.

The meal was a roast with greens and baby potatoes and crisp salad and several bottles of red Zinfandel from Sonoma County. Over coffee, Tyrone stood up to make an announcement.

'Miss Jones has agreed to do me the honor of becoming my wife.'

Applause, handshakes, kisses, tears.

Mary said, 'The only condition I insisted on was that I choose all the music for the wedding.'

Laughter and more applause.

After dinner, Mary and Masani cleared the table while Tyrone, Hakeem, and Lindsey retreated to the living room to talk about the current basketball playoffs and the coming baseball season. That much, at least, was pure tradition.

It was raining harder than ever, and a westerly wind howled through the trees. Eventually Hakeem and Masani, Tyrone and Mary, Jamie and Tanya took their leave.

Lindsey faced Marvia Plum as they sat on the couch. 'I'll call a cab,' he said. 'It was a wonderful evening. The meal. The family. I guess . . . '

'What, Bart?'

'Since you and I, Marvia . . . well, and now that Mother is remarried and, and she seems to be doing so well. She was a widow for more than forty years. I'll be honest, I had serious doubts. But it's been a good marriage for her. I've visited them down in Carlsbad and they're living in a modern condo; I've never seen her so happy.'

'Bart, you never found anyone, did you?'

He gave a wry shake of his head. 'A couple of times I thought I had. But it never quite happened. I guess I'm glad. It wouldn't have worked. And the past few years, since I got my pension, I thought I was happy. Or at least, not unhappy.'

'That's not the same thing.'

'I know.'

They were sitting on the couch, holding hands like an old-fashioned courting couple.

'It's been wonderful,' Lindsey said. 'I ought to go.'

'You could have another cup of coffee. Or a glass of wine.'

'It was very good wine.'

There was a momentary pause, then, 'Bart, stay over.'

'It's too late, Marvia.'

'No, it isn't.'

'You're just being kind.'

Her smile was wistful. 'I planned this all along.'

He released her hands and put his arms around her.

★   ★   ★

Lindsey woke up in the middle of the night and heard her breathing. The rain had lessened and a streetlamp on Bonar provided shifting illumination through branches and leaves that moved in the wind. He touched her gently, not wakening her, and pressed his face to her shoulder, and listened to her heartbeat, thinking about what he'd once had and lost, and had now regained, at least for this one night.

In the morning they faced each other across eggs and juice in a sunlit kitchen. It took Lindsey three attempts to get the words out but he finally did. 'Marvia, marry me.'

She laughed. Then she said, 'You mean it.'

'Yes.'

'Oh, Hobart, last night was lovely. This morning is fun. Here we are playing Mister and Missus, aren't we? But we're just playing, aren't we?'

'We don't have to be.'

She stood up and circled the table and pressed her cheek against his. Then she picked up a spoon and held it like a mirror. 'You're still a boy at heart, aren't you? I think most men are, all their lives. Some nice lady invites you into her bed and by morning you decide you're in love forever. That's the way a fifteen-year-old thinks.'

'I am in love with you forever.'

The toaster popped and she added toast and marmalade to their breakfast.

14

Red turned over and swung her feet from the side of the bed and onto the floor. It was cold. She tried not to waken Bobby, but he grabbed her wrist and demanded, 'Where you goin'?'

'Nowhere, Bobby. Nowhere.'

'God damn it, where you goin'?'

'I need to take a leak, that's all.'

'All right, hurry up, damn you. The bed's gettin' cold. Not that you do me much good anymore, but at least you generate a little body heat.'

She pulled on her jeans and T-shirt and shuffled down the hall to the bathroom.

It had rained hard during the night. The wind and the sheets of icy water crashing against the window, the cold air that got in around the cracks, reminded her of that one awful night, the worst night of her life, the night she'd finally found a car to crawl into only to face that ancient geezer coming out of the house.

She could remember what he looked like, his face lit by the streetlamp, puzzled and sleepy and furious and a couple of other things that she didn't even have names for, any more than she had a name for herself except Red. And when he pulled open the car door — why the hell hadn't she had the brains to lock the door before she tried to go to sleep! — when he pulled open the car door and reached for her, she could see just what was going to happen. He'd call the cops and they'd drag her down to Martin Luther God-damn King Junior, and hold her there, and maybe it would mean another trip to juvenile hall with all the apprentice lesbians to fight off, and then back home to Mommy and Daddy who would take her to another goddamned shrink, and she'd wind up in another fancy prison for rich kids called a school, and she didn't think she could take that again.

Not again.

'Bobby,' she said.

'Shut up, I'm sleeping.'

'You're not, you're awake.'

He gave her half a shove, half a punch.

Jumping out of bed, she said, 'Ouch, Bobby. Bobby, I need a jolt.'

'We don't have anything in the house. And if we did, you know that stuff is for sale. I'm trying to run an honest business here, not a candy store for a scrawny chicken like you.'

'I'm sorry, Bobby. I'm sorry. Couldn't I have maybe just one jellybean? I need a jolt.' She was crying. She hadn't wanted to cry — she knew that Bobby got mad when she cried; but she couldn't help it. 'One little jellybean, Bobby.'

'Hell, Red, we don't have anything in the house. Can't you get that through your feeble brain?'

'But, Bobby . . . ' She was crying harder but at least he didn't hit her this time, so maybe he really did like her, she thought. Maybe he loved her. Maybe he did.

'Tell you what, Red. We'll go see Morty up in El Cerrito. I'll see if I can get anything on credit. Bastard at the Ruby Red always wants money. Cash on the barrelhead, he calls it. They must have called it that back in the ice age when he was young. But I'll try and get something on the come.'

'Thank you, Bobby.'

'Get back in bed and warm me up.'

* * *

'I'm getting somewhere, Dorothy. In fact, I'm getting a lot of somewhere, but I think I'm going to need some help.'

Dorothy Yamura leaned back in her leather chair. She wore plain clothes, but the plaque on her desk showed a pair of captain's silver bars beside her name. 'Okay. First, fill me in on the progress. Then tell me what kind of help you need.'

Marvia gave her a rundown on her efforts to backtrack the stolen laptop.

'You mean Mr. Lindsey gave us some real help, and that he and Officer Rossi actually recovered the computer?'

'That's right. Mr. Lindsey essentially got a bead on it thanks to Rachael Gottlieb. The chain led backward to the Watkins couple, the flea market Space Cadets. Mr. Lindsey worked forward from Chocron and found the machine at Universal Data

260

Services. Or, actually, with the Chen children. We have the computer itself. It's in the evidence room.'

'Did the tech crew get anything off it?'

'Nothing useful.'

'No prints? No DNA?'

'Plenty of both. There were so many fingerprints, layers and smudges, they got nothing useful. Some DNA, but it was such a stew they had to give up on that, too.'

Yamura nodded. Then she asked, 'And what about Mr. Lindsey?'

'He's satisfied. He needed to verify the presence of a file on the computer, a novel that Gordon Simmons had just completed. That's all for a civil case, not our problem.'

Yamura nodded. 'Okay, I'll buy that. But how does that get us any closer to a solution of the Simmons murder?'

'The Watkins couple — the Space Cadets — are apparently running a legitimate business.'

'Within a slightly flexible definition of legitimate.'

'Point taken. But the question for us is,

how did they get the computer? They say they bought it, strictly a cash transaction from a John and Mary Smith.'

Captain Yamura shook her head. 'You'd think they would use a little creativity. Okay, Mr. and Mrs. Smith.'

'Obviously the names are useless and the Watkinses didn't get an address or driver's license. No real ID at all. But they did get a pretty good look at the couple, and Mrs. Watkins especially was able to describe them. The Watkinses didn't get their ages, but from their descriptions they sound like a pair of teenage runaways. I'd like to borrow Celia Varela to help me look for them.'

'Done.'

Dorothy Yamura looked pleased. 'Look, Celia might already have a file on them. That flea market was in Oakland, you say?'

'The one on 880 near the Coliseum.'

'Right. So we don't know if these kids are from Berkeley. Could be Oakland, could be anywhere.'

'True enough. I'll check the database and call around. But the Simmonses lived in Berkeley, and he was killed in Berkeley. I'd expect the perp to be a Berkeley person.'

* * *

Officer Celia Varela was in her office and she was intrigued by Marvia's story. 'I think you've come to the right place, Lieutenant.' She jumped from her chair, pulled open a file cabinet and extracted a manila folder. 'That scrawny kid with the dirty blond hair, he could be any one of dozens. Standard model runaway. I could practically give you his life story right now. But the girl — the redhead — she sounds familiar. I'm pretty sure she's been through this office, and I think I know who she is.'

She had laid the folder on her desk. She turned the folder in a half-circle and pushed it across her desk toward Marvia. There was a picture of a young girl. She looked to be junior high school age.

Marvia asked, 'How old is the picture?' Then, 'Oh, here's a date stamp on the back. Year and half ago.' She studied the personal data and history in the file. 'They certainly start young these days, don't they?'

'You have any of your own, Lieutenant? If you don't mind my asking.'

Marvia smiled. 'Just one.'

'No problems?'

'You're kidding, of course. He did well. Worst problem I ever had with him was over smoking weed. You know what I heard. 'All the kids are doing it, Ma, and besides, you drink booze and weed is no worse, and look at the tobacco ads all over the place, and we know how much damage that does and how addictive it is.' And the thing is, of course, he was totally right.'

'So what did you do?'

'I had to fall back on 'The law is the law, and when you're grown up you can try and change it.' That plus, 'Because I'm your mother.''

Varela laughed. 'I have three little ones.'

'Enjoy them while you can, Celia.'

'But what about your son?'

'Big shot at Pixar. Planning to be married soon. Someday I expect they'll have a couple of sprouts of their own. Then I'll play the doting grandma. I can't wait.' She turned the pages in the case folder on the desk. 'Familiar story, isn't it? We pick her up, Mommy and Daddy take her home, she gets in trouble again and we start all over again.'

'Except this one has been on her own for over a year. Parents come to see me every so often and I can't give them much more than sympathy. They have plenty of bucks. Hired a private detective, even. Kellen Jamison.'

'I know him. Used to be a cop in San Francisco. Took a bullet and a pension and went into business for himself. He have any luck?'

Varela shook her head. 'Only of a negative nature. He's pretty sure young Miss Horton isn't in the city or up in Marin. He keeps changing his story. One day she's in LA. Next day she's in Berkeley, Oakland, Alameda.'

Marvia closed the folder and handed it back to Varela. 'They might be able to give us something at juvenile hall. It's a nice day. Let's take a ride.'

They tried to make it look like a school, but the minute you laid eyes on Alameda County Juvenile Hall in San Leandro, you knew it was a prison. A temporary prison for runaways, substance abusers, under-age prostitutes, arsonists, gang-bangers and killers. Capacity, 299 juveniles. Present population, 425 and counting. They would stay here for a few hours or a few days, sometimes a lot longer than that, before a court remanded them to a longer-term facility or sent them home to Mommy and Daddy.

The sheriffs deputy who greeted Marvia and Celia was plump and looked almost young enough to be an inmate. Her tan uniform, in contrast to the others' police midnight-blue, made her look more like a Girl Scout. She had prepared for their arrival and had Juvenile Hall's version of the case folder on her desk, neatly squared away, ready for examination.

'Here it is, Lieutenant, Officer. Not very much more than I could have told you on the telephone.'

'I know that,' Marvia told her. 'But I think somebody out here might give us something more.' The folder contained the same photo she had seen in Celia Varela's office. There were fingerprints. Those would be the same. 'Horton, Rebi,' Marvia commented. 'Unusual first name.'

'Hebrew,' the deputy said. 'It's a variant of Rivka or Rebeccah.'

'You know a lot about names.'

'A hobby of mine.'

Marvia consulted the folder once more. 'Parents' address, nice neighborhood. Wish I could live like that. And look at those schools she's been in and out of. And her arrest and custody record.' She shook her head. 'How can a girl from that kind of home compile this kind of biography by the age of fifteen?' She closed the folder. 'All right, I want to talk to somebody who knows her. Teachers, therapists, anybody who can help me.'

The deputy nodded. 'I've got just the person for you. Our best drug person.' She picked up a telephone and punched a couple of numbers. 'Kyoko? You have a few minutes to discuss one of your cases?

I've got a couple of Berkeley police officers here. Okay.' She turned to Marvia. 'She'll be right here. Dr. Kyoko Takakura.'

Dr. Takakura was slim, looked forty, and dressed casually. She shook hands all around. 'I hope one of my girls isn't in trouble again,' she said.

'I'm afraid she may be, but mainly we want to find her,' Marvia explained.

'Name?'

'Rebi Horton.'

The sheriff's deputy passed the folder to Takakura. She looked at the photo and scanned a few lines of data. 'Oh, yes. Little Red.' She looked around and slipped into a chair. 'She and I are getting to be old friends. What can I tell you about her?'

'Give me a breakdown: what's her situation, what can I expect, where is she likely to turn up?'

Takakura shrugged and turned her hands up. 'Mars? Los Angeles? Maybe — best we can hope for, I think — back here. And that wouldn't be good news. It would just be less bad than the alternatives.'

'What's her drug of choice?'

'Well, as a one-time musician client of mine used to say, just tell her how to use it. Drink it, smoke it, shoot it, snort it, or shove it up her butt.'

'Oh my god.'

'Well, except — ' She studied the folder again briefly. ' — it's been a while, and I need to refresh my memory. Okay. She's mainly a pill freak. I see a note here in my own handwriting; she calls them jolts, or jellybeans. Always wants another jellybean. She'll take uppers or downers, but she prefers uppers. Apparently she never got into smoking crack, which is very good news, and she doesn't like needles so she doesn't shoot up, which is also good.'

'Anything she especially likes?' Marvia asked.

'Well, there's a sort of gray-market drug, the kids call it zing. That's not the commercial name, but that's their word. And of course good old crystal meth; she's been known to smoke that. Likes oxycontin, likes tramadol, likes vicodin. But she likes uppers better than downers.'

Another glance at the file folder. How many cases did Takakura have to carry?

'You know about Adderall?' Takakura asked.

'That's a new one on me,' Marvia said.

Dr. Takakura looked pained. 'Trouble is, this one is a legitimate prescription drug. It's been approved for treatment of narcolepsy and attention deficit disorders in both children and adults. There have been some good results with school-age children. Our Miss Horton started using it at age eleven, courtesy of Mom and Dad. But she got to like it too much and started supplementing her dosage with her generous allowance.'

'You'll have to fill me in.'

'All right. At the risk of too much information — this stuff is basically amphetamine plus dextroamphetamine, with a couple of other minor additives. It stimulates production of norepinephrine in the brain. Unfortunately it can have some nasty side effects. If you've been taking monoamine oxidase inhibitors like isocarboxazid or tranylcypromine, the stuff will probably kill you. But those things are mainly used in Parkinson's patients, so Miss Horton has probably never even heard of them.' She drew a breath. 'But Adderall itself can cause dizziness, insomnia, headaches, diminution of appetite, weight loss . . . and of course, the stuff is addictive in its own right. Some of the kids, like Rebi, call it jolt.'

Marvia was taking that in. 'When did you last see Rebi Horton?'

'Little over a year ago.'

'How about her family situation?'

'Rich mommy and daddy. Rebi's their only child. They try to give her everything. Tried. I think they mean well, but they are totally, totally clueless.'

Marvia and Celia Varela exchanged looks. Marvia asked if Takakura had any idea where Rebi might be now, and what she would be doing.

'If her parents haven't sent her off to a locked-ward so-called school in Utah or Switzerland or wherever,' she said, 'and if she's still alive?'

'Yes.'

'Probably hooking.'

'But all that money . . . why would she need to hook for a living?'

Takakura smiled. 'You're not going to

catch me on that one, Lieutenant. You know better than that. This is a kid who's so full of rage, she would do anything to hurt her parents. She wanted to be a regular kid and they wanted her to be their special princess. You remember that Boulder case years ago, that six-year-old pageant queen who was murdered?'

'Of course.'

'Rebi Horton wasn't pushed and molded like that. What happened to that poor Ramsey girl was pure child abuse, long before whatever sick pervert killed her. But Rebi's parents just kept prodding their little girl to be what they wanted her to be. They didn't give a good goddamn what *she* wanted to be. This is the result.' She sighed. 'If they get their hands back on her, I'll tell you right now, that child is doomed. I shouldn't say this, Lieutenant. This is off the record, but it's the truth. And if they don't get her back . . . well, there's maybe one chance in a hundred that she'll wake up one morning before it's too late, and look in the mirror, and see what she's made out of herself and ask for help.'

'One in a hundred?'

'I'm a hopeless optimist, Lieutenant Plum. Utterly hopeless.'

15

'Get dressed, stupid. If you want your jolt so bad, I'll get you a jolt. But you have to work for it. Come on.'

Bobby slipped into his jeans and shoes. He wore an Oakland Raiders T-shirt and a bright red American Red Cross baseball cap that must have blown off some chump's head during a storm and gone skittering along the sidewalk, straight to Bobby.

'We'll go up to El Cerrito and talk to Morty at the dog.'

'That's good, Bobby. Morty always has plenty of jellybeans. We can always sell his stuff at the schools.'

Bobby pulled on his boots and grunted. He stood up and squeezed Red's elbow.

'But, Bobby,' she said, 'you told me that Morty only takes cash. We don't have any cash, do we?'

'Not yet.' He opened the dresser drawer where Red knew he kept his Marine Hunter knife and his Beretta revolver. He stood over the dresser, studying the drawer. Finally he turned around. 'You ain't been poking in here, have you? I warned you, keep your mitts off this drawer and your nose out of here. I warned you, Red!'

He backhanded her, but only once, and only medium hard. She'd been hit much harder than that before. So she smiled at him. 'Never.'

He removed the knife and its sheath from the drawer and slipped them into his jeans pocket.

They caught a ride on University, down to the freeway and up the freeway to El Cerrito, then another up to San Pablo. Walked past a grocery store where they sampled a few grapes and cherries from open bins. In one corner of the store, a woman in a chef's hat was handing out free samples of beef stew and French bread that made a nice little meal along with free lemonade and coffee. The customers, a mixture of yuppies and welfare mamas, gave them dirty looks, and the chef handing out the free samples didn't seem any too pleased to see them, but nobody made an issue of their freeloading, and Bobby and Red left the store happy.

On the way out they passed the row of cashiers giving balloons to little kids riding in shopping baskets. Red asked Bobby if he thought she could get a balloon, and he hustled her out of the store before they attracted any more attention than they already had.

A gas station. A sporting goods store. An animal hospital, where they treated animals better than they did human beings. Red stopped and watched people bringing their pets in and out of the establishment. 'I had a dog,' she told Bobby. He didn't answer. She said, 'I could work in a place like that. I love animals. I could wash dogs. I could be a helper. Maybe someday I could — '

She stopped talking and started to cry. Right there, standing in the sunlight on the sidewalk in front of an animal hospital, bawling.

'Someday what?' Bobby said. 'You want to wash dogs for a living?'

'I don't know. They have schools. They teach you how to take care of animals. I could be an animal doctor. A veterinarian.' She pronounced the last word slowly, hitting every syllable with care.

'Yeah, someday. Let's go, it's hot in the sun.'

'I could use a jolt,' Red said.

'Walk.'

A paint store. A pizzeria.

'Bobby, I don't feel so good.'

'We're nearly there.'

The Ruby Red Pup was open. It opened early, catering to pensioners with nothing better to do than hang out, nursing their drinks, telling each other the same stories they'd been telling each other for the past decade. The neon dog in the bar's window glowed darker than blood. The upper half of the Dutch door was open and a couple of grizzled customers were leaning out, smoking.

Bobby told Red to wait outside. He pushed the lower half of the Dutch door open wide enough to squeeze through. It was dark inside the Pup and the odor of stale tobacco smoke permeated the establishment, revenant of the days before the health Gestapo had pushed through the indoor smoking ban for bars and restaurants.

Morty was behind the bar, red jacket matching the neon dog in the window, gray ponytail hanging over his collar. He was teaching a new relief man the layout. He looked up when Bobby came into the place, and frowned. 'What do you want, kid? You know you're not allowed in here. You want me to lose my license?'

'I gotta talk to you, Morty.'

'Why? You think I got time for every punk kid who wanders in here? You looking for a handout? Go try Jolly Mussolini's Pizza. They always have leftovers.'

'I gotta talk, Morty.'

Morty heaved a dramatic sigh. The new relief man was washing glasses. Morty tapped him on the shoulder. 'Keep an eye on the customers. I'll be right back.' He signaled Bobby with a follow-me gesture and headed for the back room.

Bobby waited for Morty to shut the door and click the latch into place. 'I need some merchandise, Morty.'

'Big surprise.'

'Any kind of jolts. Business is good

these days. I guess it's the season.'

'You're right, fella. Only time of year they want junk is summer, winter, spring, or fall. How much do you need?'

'What can you give me?'

'What can you pay for?'

'I'll have plenty of money, Morty. You know that. One quick round of the schools and I'll pay you for everything and have money to buy more.'

'You mean you got no dough.'

'Did I say that?'

'Show me the money, Bobby. You know there's no credit in this business.'

Somebody knocked on the door and Morty's relief man said, 'You better look at this, Mort.'

Morty unlatched the door and opened it about a foot. The relief man was standing there, still wearing his apron. A scrawny girl was struggling to get away from him. 'Went for the Slim Jims, and when I grabbed her she came around the bar and headed for the register.'

The girl was kicking and screaming. Behind her the regulars were drifting toward the exit.

'Jesus Christ, let her in and go back and tell the customers everything is okay.'

The relief man said, 'Right,' and complied. He returned to his customers, closing the back-room door behind him.

Red collapsed on the floor. 'Morty,' she sobbed.

He shook his head. 'Bobby, how many times have I told you, keep this kid out of here? Bad enough if the state people or the local cops see you around here, but this piece of jailbait would be a complete train wreck.' He stood over Red. 'Get up. Can you get up? Can you stand up?'

He leaned over to help Red to her feet. She took his arm, clutching his forearm through the red bartender's jacket with one hand, digging her fingernails into the back of his hand with the other. She made it halfway off the floor, tugged again and lunged for his eyes with her fingernails.

At the same time Bobby let him have it on the back of the head with a bottle of Gilbey's Gin. Morty went down like a sack of sand. Bobby had his Marine Hunter knife out. He grabbed Morty by the ponytail and pulled him off Red and swiped the Marine Hunter across the front of Morty's throat.

Red rolled sideways, avoiding part of the gush of blood from Morty's jugular. She staggered to her feet and started to cry.

Bobby scrambled to the door and latched it to keep the relief man out. He turned and stood over Morty. Morty's blood had covered an area in the middle of the room, with Morty himself lying face down in the middle of the dark red pond. Morty actually groaned once, blood bubbling from his throat, and twitched. His hands were stretched in front of him and the fingers quivered a couple of times, and then he didn't do anything else.

Red was making weird squeaking noises and twitching movements, crossing and uncrossing her hands in front of her face.

Bobby told Red to shut up. There was a bathroom just off the bar's storage room with a sink and a toilet and a rusty shower that dripped steadily. He half dragged, half carried Red in there, pulled her clothes off her, and shoved her in the shower, and turned both knobs on full force. The drip turned to a lukewarm trickle. He scrubbed the blood off her with an old brush that he found. By the time she was as clean as she was going to be, he'd got the blood off himself as well. He found a stack of bar mops and dried her off the best he could and ordered her to crawl back into her clothes again.

Biggest problem now was the chance that Morty had moved his stock of pills since last time Bobby was here. But he hadn't, the stupid jerk. Bobby threw everything he could find, not just pills but other stuff, into a corrugated cardboard carton. He even took the bottle of Gilbey's. Then he grabbed Red by the wrist and dragged her out the back door, the cardboard carton under his other arm. They jumped off the wooden loading dock, scrambled past a couple of garbage bins, a rusting, overflowing Dumpster and a pile of old tires, and started to run.

They headed further up San Pablo, toward Richmond. Bobby dragged Red across the wide avenue at a traffic light near a freeway ramp.

They sat together on a bus bench, but the buses didn't stop as they passed. Just as well. *We're rich*, Bobby thought. He took one look inside his corrugated box and grinned happily, and then folded down the four cardboard rectangles to keep the box closed. *We're rich, except we don't have any money. Once we move the merchandise, though, we'll be set but good.*

He got to his feet, pulled Red up beside him, walked her to the curb and put out his thumb.

* * *

Carolyn Horton left the Lexus in a commercial parking lot on Piedmont Avenue and walked the rest of the way to Kaiser Hospital. As she headed for Joseph's room, she recognized Claudia Chen hurrying down the corridor. She called her name and Doctor Chen stopped and gave her an I-should-know-you-but look.

'I'm Carolyn Horton. My husband — '
'Oh, yes. Mrs. Horton.'

'Doctor, how is he? I came to visit.'

Dr. Chen took a minute to sort through the cases in her mind. 'I'm a little worried, Mrs. Horton.'

'But you said . . . you said no vital organs were damaged. You said he would recover.'

'I still think so. I don't mean to alarm you.' Dr. Chen looked at her wristwatch. 'I only have a minute. I'm expected in — never mind. Come over here. Sit down and I'll be as fast as I can.'

There was another of those waiting rooms where exotic fish distracted terrified family members, or tried to.

'Your husband has a concussion, but not a severe one, and the knife wound could have been a lot worse than it was. That's the good news. The bad news is, apparently the knife wasn't very clean. We don't know exactly what kind of bacteria were on it, but there was something pretty nasty. Methicillin-resistant staphylococcus aureus. It's a particularly dangerous bacterium. It's very hard to treat and it can lead to septicemia. It's potentially fatal. Your husband is on massive doses of an antibiotic cocktail: penicillin, cipro-floxacin and clindamycin. Penicillin is one of our oldest antibiotics and it's still the medication of first choice. The others are much more recent, and they're two of our most powerful antibiotics.'

'Then he'll recover. He'll be all right.'

'We hope so.'

'Is he conscious? Can I see him?'

'I don't see why not.'

Carolyn Horton got to her feet. 'Doctor, is this — ' She couldn't find the word.

'Mersa.'

'Yes. Is it contagious? Will I get it?'

'Wash your hands thoroughly before you touch your husband and again afterward. You should be all right.' Dr. Chen hurried away, almost running to her next meeting.

Carolyn Horton reached into her purse, came up with her cell phone, and placed a call. She ended the brief conversation with, 'All right. Please hurry.' She went on to her husband's room. He was lying on his back, a bandage around his head and, she knew, another on the wound in his back. He did not look good. His eyes were closed, his skin had a pallid appearance, and his breathing was ragged.

She washed her hands thoroughly, as Dr. Chen had instructed, using the antiseptic soap she found in the adjacent bathroom. She touched her husband on the shoulder, making contact only with his hospital gown and not his flesh. He stirred and made a vague sound. She shook him by the shoulder and he opened his eyes, looking puzzled. Then his expression changed to one of recognition.

'Carolyn?'

'I'm here, Joseph. How are you feeling?'

Long pause. 'Lousy. My back hurts and my head hurts and I just feel totally lousy. And what's this?' He looked up at the IV bottle that was feeding a steady drip into his arm. 'How's — ' He drew a deep breath. When he'd exhaled he started again. 'How's Rebi?'

'I don't know, Joseph. I don't know where she is.'

'I thought . . . oh, I forgot. I was thinking . . . They've got me on morphine, you know.'

'No, I didn't know that. I saw Dr.

Chen. She says you're on antibiotics. I forget their names. Antibiotics. Everything sounds like science fiction. She didn't mention morphine.'

'Miserable stuff. It makes my mind . . . I can't think straight. What did you say, how's Rebi doing?'

'Joseph, you were the last one to see her. Don't you remember? You went looking for her and you claim that you saw her on MacArthur Boulevard before someone hit you from behind.'

For several minutes Joseph Horton didn't move. Carolyn wasn't sure whether he was processing what she'd just told him, or was simply in a morphine-induced fugue. She decided to push him a little. 'You took the Prius and you said you were going to look for her. You came down here to Oakland and you wound up in Kaiser.'

More silence, but then, 'I remember. Yes. There was a police officer here and a district attorney. They threatened to arrest me as a child molester.'

'Thank heaven that didn't happen!'

'Is she safe?' he asked.

'I don't know, Joseph. But she's alive. At least I think she's alive. But that's what I want to talk to you about.'

The door swung open and a broad-shouldered individual limped into the room. 'Mrs. Horton. Mr. Horton.' He offered a tentative smile.

'Mr. Jamison,' Carolyn greeted him.

'I came as soon as I could. I was on a stakeout. There was . . . well, never mind the details. It was sordid but it's a living. Anyway, I got a man in to take over. What can I do to help?'

Carolyn nodded toward her husband. 'He says he saw her.'

'Rebi — really? Mr. Horton, what about that?'

Joseph Horton muttered something unintelligible.

Carolyn said, 'They've got him on morphine. I don't think he knows if he's awake or asleep.'

Kellen Jamison pursed his lips. 'Maybe you could tell me, then.'

'He says he was looking for her on MacArthur. Over there somewhere.' She gestured vaguely toward the freeway.

'Hot-sheet row. All right. And then?'

'He claims he saw her. He parked the Prius and ran after her. She was with this . . . man, and — '

'Either a pimp or a john. Possibly an undercover cop. Did your husband get a good look at him?'

'Not much. He was concentrating on Rebi.' She told him the story.

Jamison rubbed his jaw with a callused hand. 'What do you think, Mrs. Horton?'

'About his story? I don't know. He might be hallucinating. It might have been some other child who bore a resemblance to Rebi. Or it might have been her. What do you think, Mr. Jamison?'

He shook his head. 'No way of telling. But it's a definite possibility. No question, it bears following up.'

'You think she might actually be staying in one of those horrible places?'

'She might have been but she certainly isn't now. After a violent incident and police involvement, that's the last place she'd be. It's possible that her pimp got her out of town. Or, more likely, he's got her hidden away in some safe place.

Someplace that's as safe as he can get her.'

Carolyn Horton pressed her hands to her cheeks. 'I don't know what to do now.'

'Mrs. Horton, that's what you've got me for. Now's the time to turn up the heat.'

16

Kellen Jamison stepped closer to Joseph Horton's bed.

'Don't touch him,' Carolyn Horton commanded.

'Is he conscious?'

'Never mind. We need to talk.'

They headed for a lounge. They sat on ugly plastic armchairs. Carolyn said, 'If he really saw Rebi, we may be able to find her.'

'I agree. Nothing else has worked very well. I've talked with the Berkeley police and I'm pretty sure that she has a male partner. If your husband really saw her on MacArthur, and I'm inclined to think that he did, then she's engaged in prostitution.'

Carolyn clutched her purse tightly, her fingers whitening with stress. She bit her lip but did not interrupt Jamison.

'Her partner works as her procurer. That's what was going on the night your husband was attacked. But I've been doing some surveillance at the schools in Berkeley. There's a major trade in drugs there. Everything from the old standbys to the latest invention. But the biggest items are prescription drugs. Kids steal them from their parents, or they get prescriptions for themselves, and they peddle them to their classmates.'

'Rebi wouldn't do such a thing.'

'Mrs. Horton, you know the old saying, 'Never say never.' Of course your little flower would do that. Given the right motivation, anybody will do anything. That's the way of the world. I was a San Francisco cop for twenty-two years, and believe me, I saw things that would curl your hair. Things I would never have imagined until I saw them with my own eyes.'

She opened her Versace purse and found a handkerchief. Jamison waited until she'd finished crying. She wiped her eyes and nose, and closed the purse on the handkerchief. 'I should go and fix myself up,' she said.

'That can wait.'

'Mr. Jamison, for all the money my

husband pays you, you haven't done much. You haven't found my daughter.'

'There are no guarantees in this business, Mrs. Horton. If you want me to stop I'll submit a final report and invoice. Just say the word.' He got to his feet.

She clung to her purse with one hand and clutched his wrist with the other. 'No. No. We have to keep trying. You must tell me what to do. I want to help you find her.'

'All right. Here's the good news. If your husband really saw her in that hookers' parade, we know that she's alive and in the area. Or at least that she was within the past few days. The bad news is that she's spooked now. She and her boyfriend or partner or pimp. So they've probably gone to ground. That's going to make it harder than ever to locate her.'

'But then, what can we do?'

'We go back to basics. She's probably not in a crack house. Not if she mixes pill-peddling with whoring.'

Carolyn Horton shuddered. 'Do you have to use that ugly word?'

'I call it what it is. Now take a deep

breath. We don't want you in a hospital bed, too!'

She forced herself to obey. 'Thank you.'

'I have a couple of operatives looking for her. But you and I can start a little surveillance of our own. We start at the school where she'd most likely try to mingle with the kids and move her merchandise. A little foot patrol. If that doesn't work, we start moving in circles. We'll drive together, passenger and navigator. We'll be ripples in a pond, Mrs. Horton. Ripples in a pond.'

'All right. I want to see Joseph once more. Then we'll get the Lexus and start.'

But Joseph was gone from his room. The first medical worker Carolyn could stop directed her to the nearest nurses' station and the duty nurse told her that he was back in Intensive Care.

Jamison told her to go home when she'd finished her visit with her husband. He'd do the day's work, the foot patrol, alone. She was to rest. He would come by the house in the morning if nothing developed today, and they would perform what he called ripple surveillance.

★ ★ ★

'Rich and poor at the same time,' Bobby muttered.

Red couldn't make out what he was saying but she didn't want to ask him to repeat it. He got mad when she did that and she didn't want to make him mad.

She knew she'd feel better if she had a jolt, and she knew that the corrugated box that Bobby was holding was full of what she needed, full of enough jelly-beans to keep her high and happy for a very long time. She wanted to ask Bobby to let her have a jolt right then. What would he say? She'd helped him at the Ruby Red Pup; she'd distracted Morty and helped Bobby make Morty give them what they wanted.

At least that was what she thought had happened in the storeroom at the Pup. It had all happened so fast, she'd been so confused, and she really needed a jolt. Something else had happened, she thought. She held up her hands and looked at them. Her parents would have approved, they were so clean. But how had she got so clean? Her clothes were damp, drying out in the sunlight. How had they got wet?

'Bobby,' she said. 'Bobby, I need a jolt. Don't we have any in that box? A jellybean, that's all they really are. They're just candy. Just a couple of them to make me feel better.'

Before he could reply, a car pulled to the curb. Bobby looked at it. The same Beamer ragtop that they'd ridden in once before. It was really designed for two people, but Red was so skinny she hardly took up any room, and Bobby wasn't much bigger around than she was. They could share a seat and click the shoulder belt over both of them.

There was the same dude who'd given them the ride. And there was that funny vanity plate, BMRMEUP.

'Hey, kids, need another lift?'

They piled into the car. Bobby asked the dude how his visit to Santy had gone and they all had a laugh.

The guy was really nice. He asked where they were going, and when Bobby told him Acton Street in Berkeley he swung down University, cut over to Acton, and dropped them off. Bobby thanked him — Red wasn't talking — and they climbed the stairs from the musty lobby of the Van Buren to their room.

★　★　★

Getting Jack Burnside to agree to meet with Lindsey and Eric Coffman was like getting North Korea to sit down at a conference table. First Burnside wouldn't take Lindsey's phone call, then he was too busy to have a sit-down, then he was paying International Surety through the nose to cover his risks and he expected them to do their job and not bust his chops over every little uncrossed T and undotted I in his contracts. He was a publisher, not a lawyer — didn't anybody wearing a fancy suit understand that? But finally Lindsey managed to convince him.

Lindsey arrived early for the meeting and waited on the sidewalk for Eric Coffman. When Coffman showed up, he was leaning on a cane, looking more like Raymond Burr than ever. He had his associate, Kelly McGee, at his side. She was carrying the briefcase.

They rode up to Jack Burnside's Gordian House office. He greeted them grudgingly.

Suddenly Lindsey flashed again on who Burnside reminded him of. Lee J. Cobb. No question about that. Except for the fact that Cobb had always exuded a kind of gruff integrity behind his screen persona, no matter how abrasive he managed to make himself. And Burnside didn't do that. Didn't do it at all.

Coffman laid out the case that Marston and Morse and Angela Simmons had against Gordian. 'I know their attorney, Jenny Caswell. And her principal, Paula Morse. I'm sure that Mrs. Simmons will go along with whatever arrangement Mrs. Morse recommends. They're being very reasonable, Mr. Burnside.'

'They're just a bunch of arrogant intellectuals trying to put me out of business.'

'They're not trying to put you out of business at all,' Kelly McGee put in. Lindsey suspected that a signal had passed between Coffman and McGee.

Burnside said, 'If they don't want to put me out of business, why the hell don't they just leave me alone? Let 'em go ahead and publish their books about meditation or growing your own organic endives. Leave the shoot-'em-ups to me. I know how to do those things. What the hell are Marston and Morse doing with private-eye books?'

'They have every right to publish them,' Coffman came back. 'Just as you would have the right to publish books about — what did you say — meditation and organic endive cultivation.' He leaned forward on his cane and tapped his finger on Burnside's desk. 'The point, Jack, is that you published a book that belonged to them.'

'I know, *The Emerald Cat*. I wish I'd never heard of that thing. I bought it in good faith. Not my fault if the author was a crook. Or his agent. Another one of those airy-fairy new age weirdos. I should have thrown her out on her cute little tooshy the first day she showed up here with a manuscript.

'I bought the thing in good faith and it isn't my fault if Steve Damon was a plagiarist. Or whatever his name was.'

Burnside turned angrily to Lindsey. 'You've been awfully quiet this morning. What the hell does International Surety have to say for itself?'

Lindsey blinked. Lee J. Cobb with that unshaven cleft chin jutting out. 'Our attorney, Mr. Coffman here, recommends that we settle with Marston and Morse. International Surety agrees. I'm sure we can negotiate a very reasonable settlement and there will be no lawsuit.'

'Oh, really?' Burnside leaned away from the others. 'I'm not a quitter. I don't fold under pressure. That's the way I operate. It's brought me this far and I'm not changing now.'

Lindsey looked at the ceiling. Now was the time to play bad cop. It wasn't his style, and he didn't like to do it, but he would if he had to. 'If you force their hand, Marston and Morse will sue Gordian House. And if that happens, I'm sure that Mr. Coffman will mount the best possible defense, but from what I have learned, you'll probably lose. And if that happens, I can tell you right now, you will file a claim with International Surety *and International Surety will deny the claim.'*

Burnside looked as if he was ready to explode. 'Then I'll sue International Surety. The shysters will have a field day, but I'll squeeze it out of I.S.!'

Lindsey looked at Coffman and said, 'Eric, remember what you explained to me?'

Coffman looked at Kelly McGee and said, 'Miss McGee, I know you're up to speed on the concepts of due diligence and full disclosure. Would you please explain those to Mr. Burnside?'

She was, and she did. It went on for a while. Finally it looked as if Burnside had got the message. Coffman nodded to McGee, who pulled a folder out of her briefcase and removed a form. It was a memorandum covering the events of the meeting. Obviously, either she had been a Girl Scout or her employer had been a Boy Scout; in either case, they were definitely prepared.

McGee handed the memorandum to

Burnside and asked him to read it carefully and sign it.

'I don't want to sign anything.'

'We really do need it.'

He muttered and lowered his face so he could read the memorandum without actually touching it. Then he looked up and announced, 'I'm hungry. I never sign anything on an empty stomach. Never.'

Burnside shoved the memorandum away from himself. It slid off the edge of his desk and was caught in a stray air current. Kelly McGee captured it and returned it to her briefcase.

Coffman said, 'Will you excuse us for a moment, Mr. Burnside?'

They moved to the outer office, and the receptionist retreated to the editorial room that Lindsey had seen on his first visit to Gordian.

Lindsey said, 'What do you think?'

Coffman tilted his head toward Kelly McGee.

McGee said, 'Candidly, this guy is either a moron, or an overgrown brat, or a shrewd operator.'

'And what do we do? What's your

recommendation, counselor?' Coffman had brought his cane with him from Burnside's office and stood leaning on it. Lindsey was impressed by his recovery from his mugging, but still Coffman winced with pain when he moved.

'We have to stick to our guns,' McGee said. 'Mr. Lindsey, you're not going to change your position, are you? I mean, International Surety's position?'

Lindsey shook his head. 'He bought tainted goods. He published a book that belonged to somebody else. He's in a hole, and we have to make him stop digging before he hits the water table.'

They trooped back into Burnside's office. He greeted them with, 'I'm hungry.' He picked up his phone and hit a couple of buttons. 'Sandwiches. Here, everybody write down your order, my girl will call out for sandwiches.'

Waiting for the meal to arrive, Burnside left his own office. 'I've got a business to run. I'll be in Editorial. Don't anybody touch anything. I'll know if you do.'

Lindsey, Coffman and McGee exchanged shrugs and stood quietly until they heard a crash that shook the light fixtures in Burnside's office. Then Jack Burnside's roaring voice, indistinct but filled with rage, resounded from Editorial. He slammed the door open and launched himself back into his swivel chair like a wrestler landing on a helpless opponent.

'Where the hell is my lunch? I want my lunch!'

Burnside's receptionist entered the room with a covered tray. She placed it on Burnside's desk and removed the cover. Burnside tore into an overstuffed sandwich. When he'd finished the sandwich, he tugged the lid from a cardboard container. Wisps of steam and the odor of coffee emerged. Burnside slugged down its contents like a college boy chugging a can of beer. Then he threw the remnants of his meal into a wastebasket.

'Now, you sons of bitches, what's the bottom line? If I fight these brie-eaters, do I have a chance? Any chance at all? Coffman, give it to me on the level.'

Eric Coffman intoned, 'We lawyers are trained never to promise anyone anything. But if I had to make a promise, Mr.

Burnside, I would promise you this. Fight this lawsuit and you will lose.'

Burnside snarled. 'You, girlie — what's your name, MacDuff? Whatever. Does this stuffed shirt know what he's talking about? If I hire you away from him, will you fight this case for me?'

Kelly McGee kept her cool. Lindsey detected the ghost of a smile around Eric Coffman's mouth. 'I don't think I could ethically go to work for you at this point, Mr. Burnside,' she said. 'But if I were your attorney, based on what I know of the case, I would urge you to settle.'

'And you? Lindsey, what do you have to say?'

'Settle, Mr. Burnside. The other side isn't demanding unconditional surrender. Let Mr. Coffman talk to their lawyer. You'll be better off, believe me.'

Burnside jumped to his feet. He moved with remarkable speed for a man of his age and massive girth. 'All right, all right! Gulliver pulled down by the Lilliputians. You're all against me. Every one of you. All right. You, MacWhatever — you, girlie, give me the goddamned paper and

305

take it and get the hell out of my office!'

They left with the signed memorandum in Kelly McGee's briefcase. They refrained from laughing until they reached the street.

Once there, Eric Coffman said, 'I'll talk with Caswell. You'll be in town a little longer, Hobart?'

Lindsey said he would. 'In fact, I don't know — I've lived in Walnut Creek for so long, I think I might make a permanent change.'

Coffman raised his Raymond Burr eyebrows. 'Really?'

'You and Miriam happy in Emeryville?'

'I'll be honest, it took some adjusting. You don't just pull up stakes and move and go on seamlessly. But yes, we've been here a while now and no regrets.' He paused, then added, 'Miriam wanted me to invite you for dinner again. Sorry about last time, but I was otherwise detained. Not tonight, Hobart. I'm still recovering. What about some night next week? And by all means, bring your friend Marvia Plum. Miriam and I have always liked her.'

17

Kellen Jamison showed up as promised. 'Ready?' A Plymouth sedan badly in need of paint and with half its body trim missing stood at the edge of the street.

Carolyn Horton stared at the battered car and shuddered. She was holding a white leather Gucci handbag and wearing Stuart Weitzman pumps.

In the car, Jamison asked how her husband was doing.

'Not well at all, I'm afraid.'

'Sorry to hear that.'

'You will still be paid, Mr. Jamison. No need to worry about that.'

'I wasn't thinking that at all, ma'am. We're going to start at Berkeley High,' he added. 'I'm going to be driving. I'll go as slow as I can but I don't want us to be conspicuous. You keep an eye out for your daughter. If you see her, if you even see somebody you think might be her, you sound off, all right? Not to her. To me. All right?'

'I quite understand, thank you.'

'All right. If that doesn't work, I've got another idea. They need food, and there's a big outlet store down on University near the railroad tracks. A lot of people get their groceries there to save money. We'll try the school first, do ripple surveillance, and if we come up empty we'll try University.'

The conversation lapsed. Berkeley High was south of University and west of Shattuck, two of the city's main thoroughfares. By the time Jamison had covered enough territory without a sighting, he said he would try the next option. 'Gotta keep trying,' he announced.

They headed down University. The traffic was heavy. The sun beat down. The Plymouth didn't have air conditioning. It pulled to a stop at a traffic light at San Pablo Avenue.

Carolyn Horton screamed. 'I see her! I see her!'

'Where?'

'Right there,' she was crying. 'Don't you see, don't you see, right there!' She pointed ahead of them and to their left, to the south, toward Emeryville and Oakland. 'Oh, catch them, catch them!'

Traffic was flowing past them on San Pablo Avenue. They were in the wrong lane to make the turn. A truck painted with the name of a plumbing company blocked their path. Jamison leaned on the Plymouth's horn. Carolyn Horton pointed a well-manicured fingernail past him. He caught sight of a slate-gray BMW convertible, its top down. The driver wore a sporty cap. There were two figures crammed into the passenger seat, one of them a young girl with red hair. Jamison pounded his horn again and again. He even caught a glimpse of the Beamer's license tag. Long training came into play. He noted the vanity plate: BMRMEUP.

By the time the light changed, the Beamer was out of sight. It was quicker for Jamison to push on another block and circle left, back to San Pablo, hoping to catch sight of the Beamer again, but the car had disappeared.

Jamison pulled to the curb in front of a Salvation Army thrift store. Mrs. Horton sat beside him, weeping loudly.

'I saw her. She was with those two men. I saw her, I'm sure of it. Didn't I see them, Mr. Jamison? She's alive. Oh, say that she's alive.'

Jamison said, 'I think you did. We can't be certain, but from the photos you've shown me, I think that was your daughter.'

'And we lost her again. We'll never catch that little car. Oh, you should have let me take the Lexus. It's so much better than this . . . this — '

'I got the license.' Jamison opened the map compartment and fished out a pencil stub and a scrap of paper. 'I'll remember it anyhow, but just to be safe . . . ' He scribbled, 'Slate-gray BMW convertible, tag BMRMEUP.'

Carolyn turned to him and asked, 'What good will that do?'

'Lend me your cell phone, will you? I really need to get one of those things.' He punched in a number and exchanged a few words with someone. The conversation ended with, 'Holy Christ, Olaf, I'll be right there!' He handed the phone back to Carolyn. 'Go home. I can't take you. Look, grab a taxi and go home, or go

310

down to Kaiser and visit your husband. I have to hustle.'

Flustered, she tried several times to get an explanation from Jamison, but finally allowed herself to be expelled from the ramshackle Plymouth.

She hailed a cab and gave the driver her address, then set her jaw at an angry angle. Next time, whatever Kellen Jamison or anyone else said, she would use the Lexus!

Meanwhile, Jamison hit the accelerator and made it to police headquarters on MLK in record time. Olaf Strombeck met him in the lobby and they hurried to Strombeck's office in Homicide.

'Got your Beamer info from DMV. Car is registered to one Stanley G. Wilkins, residence one of those new condos on Telly near the campus. Teaches Pre-Islamic Middle Eastern History, grad level.'

'Great!'

'More than great. Listen to this: We just got a mutual aid call from El Cerrito. A really nasty 187 at the Ruby Red Pup.'

'The ruby what?'

'Ruby Red Pup. It's a bar on San

Pablo. Bartender was lured into the back room by a couple of kids. They cut his throat and left him there.'

Jamison let loose an expletive.

'But wait, there's more. Relief bartender heard the scuffle. Had to break the lock to get into the storeroom. He found the body. Throat slashed. Not sure whether the vic bled to death or choked on his own blood. Two perps got away, out the back door of the establishment. There was a little loading dock back there and they took off on foot.'

'That witness, the relief bartender . . . did he get a description of the perps?'

'You bet. Male, fifteen to seventeen, dirty blond hair, maybe five eight, hundred forty pounds. Female, thirteen to fifteen, red hair, skinny build, not much over five feet, maybe a hundred pounds. Both wearing T-shirts and jeans. And here's the best: witness says the vic knew the perps, called them Bobby and Red.'

'They're my kids! Holy Christ! What the hell were they doing in El Cerrito? What the hell?'

'Yeah, Kellen, what the hell, indeed. El

Cerrito PD says they suspected the vic, name Morty Korman, was a mid-level distributor. Anything you wanted, either Korman had it or he could get it for you, but he specialized in pills. Big man with the latest jolt, something called Adderall. It's legal with scripts but it's all the craze with the student population, college and high school, and it's working its way down to middle school.'

Jamison ran his hand across his face. 'And I just saw them. This Wilkins character — sporty type, that Beamer must have cost him fifty grand — heading down San Pablo with Bobby and Red jammed into the passenger seat.'

Sergeant Strombeck reached for the phone and punched one key. He had the UC Police on speed-dial. He shot the urgent info to his campus contact and said he'd stand by for an answer.

When it came, it came from the secretary of the chairperson of the history department. Professor Wilkins had no classes scheduled today. Nor office hours. In fact, he wasn't expected back on campus until Monday. Strombeck requested

Wilkins's home and cell-phone numbers.

He tried both and got switched twice to voicemail. He left his own number and an urgent request for a callback. Then he and Jamison went and found Captain Yamura and Lieutenant Plum in conference. He briefed them on the situation. Yamura authorized him to station a uniformed officer at Wilkins's condo and to issue an APB for Wilkins, Bobby Last-Name-Unknown, and Rebi Horton.

Yamura knew Jamison. She asked if he had any idea where Wilkins and the two suspects were headed in Wilkins's Beamer. Jamison told her that he'd seen the roadster heading south on San Pablo at University. Wilkins could have been headed for Oakland, Alameda, or points south or east of there. He had no idea what relationship existed between Wilkins and the two kids, whether the trio had remained together or separated, and in the latter case, at what point.

'Okay, Sergeant, get on the horn to the Highway Patrol. That Beamer roadster with the vanity plate should be pretty easy to spot.'

★   ★   ★

Lindsey had finished another report to Desmond Richelieu in Denver, outlining his meeting with Coffman, McGee, and Jack Burnside. The key item in the report was the fact that they'd managed to get Burnside's signature on the memorandum of agreement. Not that the paper had any legal force. Burnside could still balk at signing off on International Surety's payment to Marston and Morse, Gordian could insist on fighting the case, and if I.S. refused to stand with him, he could sue the insurance carrier. But that looked damned unlikely.

Lindsey was just about ready to wrap up the case.

He shut down his laptop, swung his feet onto the bed, and picked up the remote. Maybe he could turn up a good *noir* to while away a couple of hours.

Before he'd found anything, Richelieu responded to the report with a phone call. 'Lindsey, I can't say I'm happy with this thing. I'd hoped you'd get I.S. off the hook.'

'Sorry, Mr. Richelieu. I can't change the facts. I think we're getting away about as well as we can.'

'And I assume you're going to check out of that Taj Mahal and send in your final cheat sheet.'

'I might stay on a little longer. Personal reasons.'

'You do whatever you want to do, but as far as I'm concerned you're off the slush fund as of now, you understand?'

'Understand. And you're welcome.'

Lindsey finished hyperventilating and reached for his cell phone. He punched in Marvia Plum's cell number and felt like a schoolboy waiting for her to answer. For a moment when he heard her voice he couldn't speak. Then he asked, 'Have you had dinner yet?'

He was as tongue-tied, as restricted to banalities, as a fifteen-year-old.

She laughed, but not derisively. 'I haven't.'

'Could we — ?'

'I'm at home.'

He showered and dressed, retrieved the Avenger, and drove to her home on Bonar

Street. He didn't notice what she was wearing, only her face and her hair and a perfume far too subtle to identify but far too compelling to ignore.

He remembered a restaurant in Berkeley's Northside neighborhood, a place he hadn't visited in more than a decade. Fortunately, it was still in business. It was old-fashioned enough to have linen tablecloths and polished silver and candles on the tables. He had no idea what they ordered or what they drank, only that he kept trying to ask Marvia to marry him and suffering a failure of nerve again and again.

Afterwards, sitting in the front seat of the Avenger, he took her in his arms like a smitten sophomore and said, 'Marvia, marry me.'

It was so simple, and he felt his heart racing until she said, equally simply, 'Yes, Bart. I will.'

★   ★   ★

Olaf Strombeck felt the phone vibrating, dragged himself into wakefulness, and reached for the cell phone. 'I know, I know. Go back to sleep.' He took the phone into the living room and closed the bedroom door.

'This is Stan Wilkins. You're the police?'

'Sergeant Strombeck.'

'Sorry to bother you at this hour.'

Strombeck turned on a lamp. The clock on the mantel showed a few minutes before one. 'Is this Professor Wilkins?'

'I said so. What is it?'

'Are you in your apartment, sir? In Berkeley?'

'No, goddamn it, I am not. What do you want?'

'Do you have those kids with you? Bobby and Red?'

'What did you say your name was? Stromberg?'

'Sergeant Olaf Strombeck.'

'Well, Sergeant, I'm not in my condo, I'm not in Berkeley, I don't have any kids with me, I don't know what you're talking about — and to put it mildly, I am very annoyed.'

'You drive a slate-gray BMW roadster, California license tag BMRMEUP?'

'Yes, I do. You're not another Trekkie calling to talk about that vanity license, are you? I'm going to get rid of that thing. It's more trouble than it's worth.'

'Sir, please, this is official business and it's very serious. Would you mind telling me where you are and what you're doing?'

'All right. I don't like this. It's an invasion of privacy. But all right. I am at the Seven Gulls Inn in Santa Cruz. I am here with my wife. We've been separated and we decided to try for a reconciliation and we are having a romantic weekend getaway for two and I foolishly decided to check my cell phone for messages before getting into bed and I found your message.' He stopped, probably to get his breath. Then he said, 'Would you tell me what the hell this is all about?'

'Yes, sir. I'm sorry to bother you. Here's the situation, Professor. There was a serious crime this afternoon in El Cerrito. Someone lured a man into the storeroom of a tavern called the Ruby Red Pup and murdered him. In a particularly distressing way, I might add.'

'I'm sorry to hear it,' Wilkins said, 'but things like that are police business. I'm an academic, not a crime-fighter.'

'Sir, your car was seen headed south on San Pablo Avenue in Berkeley shortly after the crime was committed. Our witness says that two young people, a male and a female, were crowded into the passenger seat of your car. Is this correct? Does this agree with your recollection?'

There was a lengthy silence. Then Strombeck could hear a mature-sounding female voice in the background, but he couldn't understand what the woman was saying. Wilkins replied, also incomprehensibly. Then he said, 'Sergeant, that changes things. I'm sorry. What can I do to help?'

'Can you verify that you had two passengers in your car?'

'Yes. A couple of kids. Teenagers. They were hitchhiking. I happened to give them a ride a few days ago. I recognized them and thought I'd give them another lift.'

'Would you describe them, please?'

'As you said. The boy was about fifteen, dark blond or light brown hair, skinny.

Girl was maybe thirteen. Thin as a rail. Red hair, cropped short, looked like an amateur job.'

Strombeck asked, 'Was there anything else notable about them? Anything unusual?'

'They were carrying a corrugated cardboard box. I was curious about it. They said they had a sick dog at home, and they were bringing food and medicine for it.'

'Anything else?'

Another silence. Then Wilkins said, 'There was one odd thing. The girl was wet.'

'Wet? Perspiring?'

'No, not at all. She . . . her hair and face were wet. As if she'd been swimming and then got dressed without drying off first. So her clothes were damp. Or wet from the inside out.'

'Where are they now?'

'I dropped them off where they asked me to. They thanked me for the ride and I kept on going. That was all.'

'Dropped them off where, Professor Wilkins?'

'Let me think . . . yes. Acton Street. You know Acton Street in Berkeley?'

'Yes, sir. Acton and where?'

'I don't remember the cross street, maybe Addison, I'm not sure. But it was an old hotel. I think it's a boarding house now. An old hotel. The Van Buren Hotel.'

'Do you recall what time that was?'

'Around three o'clock, give or take. I wasn't keeping close track of the time. I'd taken my last class for the day and I just wanted to get back to my condo and pack my bag and head down here. Even dropping the kids off on Acton took me out of my way, but I felt sorry for them.'

'Thank you, Professor. Just one more thing, sir. When will you be back in Berkeley? We may need to talk with you again.'

'Monday, Sergeant. I have a nine a.m. on Monday.'

'Thank you, sir. Have a happy weekend. Please apologize to your wife for me.'

18

Carolyn Horton pushed the sleep mask from her eyes and reached for the bedside telephone. She knew even before the caller asked if this was indeed she; knew who was calling and what the message would be.

'Mrs. Horton, this is Father Wyshinsky at Kaiser Hospital in Oakland. I'm the chaplain on duty. I'm calling about your husband. I think you'd better get down here quickly.'

'Father Wyshinsky?'

'Yes, ma'am.'

'What kind of father is that?'

'Roman Catholic, Mrs. Horton. From the Diocese of Oakland.'

'There must be some mistake. We're not Catholic.'

'Doesn't matter, ma'am. We work in rotation. I just happened to pull the duty tonight. Mrs. Horton, I don't mean to be discourteous, but I really think you ought to hurry.'

'Couldn't it wait till morning, Mr. Wyshinsky?'

'I really don't think so, ma'am.'

She returned the handset to its cradle. The hallway fixture cast a thin light into her bedroom. She turned on a lamp and crossed to her closet, setting out to select an appropriate wardrobe.

Before long she was ready to examine her appearance in the three-way mirror she had made Joseph install in her bedroom. She knew it would be a damp, chilly night and she had selected her wardrobe accordingly.

When she got to Broadway and Mac-Arthur, the local businesses had all shut down for the night. A thin mist hung in the air, creating nimbuses of red and green around the traffic lights and pale orange around the streetlamps. There was not much vehicular traffic, and what there was moved slowly due to the limited visibility.

She strode through the lobby. She knew where she was going. She hated hospitals. They were places of sickness and death. They were almost as bad as nursing homes, where every face she saw only reminded her of her own fate, of the fate that drew closer every day. Of age and death.

At the ICU she was met by a portly silver-haired man in a business suit and by a stranger in medical garb. The silver-haired man took her hand. 'Mrs. Horton? I'm Szymon Wyshinsky. We spoke earlier.'

'I told you, we're not Catholic.'

'Of course. If you wish, we have representatives of other faiths on staff. We're all on call, twenty-four seven.'

'No. Never mind — I don't want to talk to you, I want to talk to the doctor.' She addressed a dark-skinned man with gray-shot hair. 'Are you the doctor in charge here?'

'Dr. Rosen. Yes, ma'am. I've been treating your husband.'

'Where's that woman, that Chen woman? I thought she was in charge.'

'She's off duty, ma'am.'

'Well, what about Joseph?'

'I'm afraid he's not doing well. That's why Father Wyshinsky contacted you. We find that most people would rather receive this news from the chaplain than from medical personnel.'

'Well, never mind that. I want to see my husband.'

'You can do that.'

'How is he doing? They told me he was on the best antibiotics.'

'He is, ma'am. But we're pretty sure he's infected with a Mersa bacterium. Did Dr. Chen explain Mersa to you?'

'She certainly did. And with all the premiums we pay for medical insurance I'd expected better of this hospital.'

'I'm sorry, ma'am.' He flashed a look at the chaplain standing nearby. Then, to Carolyn Horton, 'If you want to come in now. I don't think he'll be able to speak with you. He's been comatose for the past hour or so.'

She stood at her husband's bedside. His face was gray. An oxygen feed rested on his upper lip, a tiny plastic tube in each nostril. The intravenous drip was still attached to his arm. A monitor at his bedside flashed numbers that were meaningless to her, and a green line ran jaggedly across what looked like a circular video screen.

'Joseph? Joseph?'

He did not respond.

She took his hand. Nobody had said anything to her about washing before touching the patient. She had placed her gloves carefully in her Ellington Hepburn handbag. Joseph's hand felt hot and dry. She realized with a start that she might contract the infection from him. But this doctor — what was his name, she'd met so many new people lately, her head was in a whirl, Rosen, that was his name — Dr. Rosen would surely have stopped her if there was danger in touching Joseph.

She tried again, and when he failed to respond she put his hand back on the coarse white bedsheet. She would be sure to wash thoroughly with antiseptic soap before leaving the room.

Out of the corner of her eye, she saw Dr. Rosen move toward the priest, that Father Wish-something. They put their heads together like a couple of conspirators in a bad TV movie.

'Mrs. Horton.' It was the priest. 'Mrs. Horton, I'm afraid the end is very near. Would you like me to administer last rites to your husband?'

'I told you, we're not Catholic!' She was angry.

'I don't think God would quibble, but if you'd rather — '

'No. Never mind. I told him not to go out. It's his own fault. I told him not to go out and he brought this on himself. He's a soft-bellied middle-aged business-man, and we were already paying a detective. But he had to be a hero, and now look at what he did to himself!'

She leaned over her husband, nodded, and started from the room. But she turned back and strode into the bathroom and closed the door behind herself. She washed her hands thoroughly with strong antiseptic soap and used a clean towel to handle the doorknob on her way out.

At least the Lexus had not been vandalized. In Oakland, California, in the middle of the night, any car left at the curb for more than thirty seconds was fair game for vandals.

When she got home, the light was blinking on her answering machine and the bright red readout indicated that there were two messages waiting for her. She punched the playback button to listen. The first was from that annoying Father Wyshinsky. Szymon Wyshinsky. Didn't they need priests in Poland?

'I'm very sorry, Mrs. Horton. Your husband passed away just a few minutes after you left here. I'm sure that your visit was a comfort to him. Time of death was two thirty-seven a.m. There's no need for you to do anything right now. The social worker here at the hospital will contact you in the morning to determine your wishes. Please accept my condolences, and feel free to contact me at any time.'

She slammed down on the playback button and stamped around her bedroom shaking her fists in rage. She rolled back the mirrored doors of her wardrobe. This was terrible, terrible. She was desperately understocked with black. When she had control of herself she sat down on the edge of her bed and punched the button to play the second message.

'Kellen Jamison here, Mrs. Horton. There's been an important development. Really important. And really urgent.

Please call me at once. Look, I even got myself a cell phone. Call me as soon as you get this message. If I don't answer, try Sergeant Olaf Strombeck of the Berkeley Police Department. You got a pencil? Get a pencil, I'll give you a minute to get a pencil. Okay, here's my cell number, and if you can't reach me, here's Sergeant Strombeck's number.'

She carefully wrote the numbers in her personal directory, then lifted the telephone handset and punched in Kellen Jamison's cell phone number. She didn't need to use the other number he'd given. Jamison reacted to the first ring. She announced her identity.

'Mrs. Horton, we think we've spotted your daughter. She and a companion are believed to be in a rooming house, the former Van Buren Hotel on Acton Street at Channing Way in Berkeley. Can you meet me there, absolutely ASAP?'

'But I — I've just had some very bad news, Mr. Jamison. And look at the hour. Can this wait till morning? I haven't had much sleep since my husband was attacked. And I'm really very fatigued.'

'Mrs. Jamison, it's up to you, but I think you really, really need to get down here.'

She heaved a sigh. 'Very well, Mr. Jamison. I'll come down there. I assume you'll meet me.'

'Yes, ma'am.'

She dropped the handset onto its cradle, sighed once again, and crossed the room. She opened a drawer in her signed Paul Guth chiffonier and selected a Pashmina cashmere scarf. If she had to go out again on this beastly night, she could at least dress warmly.

She pulled the Lexus to the curb, first making sure that Jamison's Plymouth was there. She also saw several black-and-white police cruisers. None of them had their lights flashing, and the street was dark and quiet.

She heard a sharp rap on the window of the Lexus and frowned angrily. Turning, she recognized Kellen Jamison. He put his finger to his lips in a ridiculously melodramatic signal for silence, then gestured, indicating that she should get out of the Lexus.

When she did, a police officer joined

them. He was very tall and good-looking in a Scandinavian way. Jamison said, 'This is Sergeant Strombeck. This is Mrs. Horton. The mother of the female juvenile.'

Carolyn Horton bristled at the use of the term 'female juvenile.' Why couldn't the man just say 'Rebi' or 'the young lady'?

Strombeck said, 'We've got a task force assembled here.' He gestured vaguely toward the police cars and the dark, ugly building half a block away. That, Carolyn assumed, was the infamous rooming house.

'We believe that your daughter and a male companion are in the Van Buren Hotel. We intend to make entry and bring them out safely if possible. But there is danger. I hope you understand that, ma'am.'

'What do you mean, bring them out? My daughter wouldn't live in such a place. Certainly not with a male companion. She's just a child.'

'Well, ma'am, we're not certain they're in there. We're trying to find out. But there may be a confrontation. We believe the young man is armed and dangerous. You might want to keep your distance, that's all.'

Marvia Plum stood facing the old cut-glass and dark wood door of the Van Buren. The lobby was dark, but her LED Tac light provided plenty of illumination. She could see the row of buzzers for the rooms in the converted hotel, but they were too small and too far to read from here. There was a single buzzer beside the outside door, a faded card beneath it reading 'Ring 4 Manager.'

She pressed the button, hoping that it still worked. She kept at it until a dark figure shuffled into the lobby. Gray hair, week's beard, sweatshirt and khakis. His expression reflected a mix of anger and sleepiness. He stood opposite Marvia, growling imprecations.

She showed him her ID. She'd decided that there was a better chance of success if she wore civvies than if she'd attempted this operation in uniform, but she knew that there were plenty of uniforms waiting in the dark to move if they were needed.

The sweat-shirted man unlocked the door. Marvia stepped inside. She signaled for silence and spoke in a soft voice. 'You have two juveniles in residence. Young female, skinny, short red hair, name is Rebi Horton. Young male, also thin, dirty blond hair, first name may be Bobby.'

'That's Bobby,' the manager said. 'Sounds like Bobby and Red. They're good kids. Quiet. Don't make no trouble.'

'All right. Are they here now?'

'How should I know? I'm not their papa.'

'You don't know, then. Is that correct?'

'Yes'm.' Getting polite now.

'Where is their room?'

'Four fourteen.'

'That's the fourth floor?'

'Yes'm.'

'There an elevator in this building?'

'No'm.'

'I see the staircase there. Is that the only one? Is there another? A fire escape?'

'No other inside stairs. Old iron fire escape on the back of the building.'

'Can they get access to that from four fourteen?'

'Could. Yes, they could.'

Marvia spoke into her shoulder radio,

relaying the information to Strombeck. Civvies or no, she was wired into her team. She spoke a few more words into the radio and waited while Strombeck joined her and the manager. Half a dozen other officers followed Strombeck. Kellen Jamison followed the police, accompanied by Carolyn Horton. A couple of uniformed officers, she knew, would be working their way up the fire escape at the back of the building.

Marvia headed up the stairs. They were carpeted. That was good; it helped her move quietly. She reached the fourth floor, cut down the setting on her Tac light, and checked the numbers on the doors. She located four fourteen. She reset the brightness on her Tac light and rapped lightly on the door.

She said, 'Rebi. Rebi, are you in there?'

She heard no reply.

She rapped harder on the door and asked more loudly, 'Rebi, are you there? Is Bobby in there with you?'

She thought she heard someone stirring.

'You need to open the door. You need

to come out. Both of you. No one will hurt you if you come out.' She had her weapon drawn.

She heard two voices, both of them sounding young: a young girl, a teenaged boy. Muttering and something that sounded like, 'All right, all right.'

A sound that might have been a drawer opening and closing. Shuffling. The two voices again, rising in volume, still unclear, a sound that might have been a blow.

The door swung open. Marvia's Tac light filled the room with a cold glare. Two figures, both of them naked, a boy and girl, and in the boy's hand something black, and there was a flash and an impact, two impacts in rapid succession, and Marvia was flung backward and off her feet, landing hard, her head crashing into something, a wall, hearing gunfire, seeing flashes and then not seeing flashes. Not seeing anything.

*   *   *

Carolyn Horton saw the door marked 414 swing open, brightness illuminate it, two figures coming toward the doorway. Two naked figures, a boy and girl. Naked, skinny, filthy. The boy held something black in his hand. A gun.

Two flashes, two booms. The black police officer facing the two crashed backward, bounced once, fell to the carpeted floor. More flashes and booms.

The boy was holding a gun in one hand, clutching the girl with the other.

Carolyn shrieked, 'Rebi, Rebi, come to Mother, Rebi!'

The girl escaped from the boy. She stumbled through the doorway. More booms. Behind the girl, a single flashing scene, blood blossoming from the boy's chest, spurting outward, the boy crashing backward into the room, disappearing from Carolyn's view.

Rebi stumbled across the body of the officer into the arms of a uniformed police-man. He lifted her and pushed his way down the hall, away from the blood and the stench of gunpowder and filth, the girl squirming in his arms like a three-year-old having a tantrum. She managed somehow to struggle free and work her way through the figures in the hallway, back to the room.

Carolyn reached for her, screeching her name. Rebi kept going, screaming obscenities, interspersed with what sounded like 'Never!'

She plunged back into the room with the bleeding boy in it, leaped over his body, onto the unmade bed, pulled the window up and climbed onto the fire escape.

More sounds of struggle, and a male voice coming from the darkness outside, something like, 'I've got her, I've got her.'

★   ★   ★

She woke to a sense of pain, but it was distant pain. Her mind was strangely clear. She tried to move, but at the first effort the pain leaped the distance and seized her, and she moaned and lay back.

She was in a hospital room, she could tell that. She even recognized the doctor; she'd seen her before — Pollyam Mukerji, the soft-spoken little Indian woman.

Marvia said, 'My baby. Is my baby all right? My Jamie. My little Jamie.'

Dr. Mukerji said, 'Marvia, you are all right. You will be all right.'

'My baby.'

She could move her eyes without turning her head. At least that didn't hurt. She could see — there were all these people in the room. Some black people, and that Japanese-looking woman, and a middle-aged white man, and the white-coated woman, the little doctor.

Dr. Mukerji turned to the others. 'This is much too great a congregation. Please go to the waiting room. One of you may stay.'

Jamie Wilkerson said, 'I'll stay.'

Everyone else started leaving. Then Marvia reached for Lindsey's hand and clutched it. So he stayed, too. Dr. Mukerji did not protest.

When there were only the three of them with Marvia, Dr. Mukerji said, 'You are Mr. Lindsey, are you not?'

'Yes,' he said.

'Mr. Lindsey, she has experienced a great insult — two bullets to the body. One smashed a rib and settled in her lung. The other went through her shoulder and exited.'

'How bad is it?'

'It is not good, but she is a strong woman. The shoulder wound, I would not say it is trivial, but it is not extremely serious. The other wound, to her lung . . . we removed the bullet and she will heal, but this is a very serious insult. She may lose the lung. But what about this baby? This Jamie?'

Jamie Wilkerson said, 'I'm her son. I'm Jamie. She must be . . . she must think she's just given birth.'

Dr. Mukerji nodded sharply, the room's fluorescent lights glinting off her glasses. 'Yes. Thank you. I am sure that is it. Under the circumstances, quite understandable.'

Lindsey and Jamie stood watch in shifts throughout the night. By noon the next day Marvia's expression indicated that her mind was clear, or as clear as it could reasonably be with her body pumped full of nutrients and antibiotics and painkillers.

She was holding Lindsey's hand. She did not speak, but her eyes indicated that she heard and followed the conversation. She pulled Lindsey's hand toward her and held it to her face. He pressed his cheek against her forehead. He placed his free hand carefully, lightly, on the hospital sheet covering her, trying mightily to send strength from his body into hers.

It would not be an easy recovery, he knew, but she would recover.

He wept with joy.

19

Six months later.

How lame could you get? The more they tried, the less it worked. Okay, so there were no bars on the windows, at least not in the would-be living rooms. Only double-thick shatter-proof glass. And a carpet on the floor that looked like it was a discard from the Bates Motel. And furniture that a bus terminal waiting room would turn down.

Magazines on the coffee table — last month's *Vogue*, a couple of old *Sports Illustrated*s, *Seventeen* for God's sake, a dog-eared *People Weekly*. She wanted to throw up. A TV in the corner, and they'd tweaked it so it only got crappy channels that nobody would ever want to look at.

Red stood gazing out the window, peering at the distant freeway, wishing she could be standing on the shoulder, thumb in the air, waiting for some trucker looking for a —

She heard the door open and turned from the window to see Kyoko Takakura come in.

'Rebi, how are you today?'

'Oh, wonderful, Dr. Takakura. Just great. I'm ready to get out of here and go back to school.'

'We have classes right here, Rebi.'

'I know.'

'You've been attending them pretty regularly. That's good. Here, won't you come away from the window and sit down and talk with me?'

'What do we have to talk about? Thank you, Dr. Takakura, is that what you want to hear? I want to thank the staff here sincerely for helping me to clean up my act, for getting my teeth fixed, for helping me to see the error of my ways so I can go forth and become a productive member of society.'

'That's good to hear, Rebi. I wish I could believe you were sincere.'

'Oh, I am, Doctor, I am very sincere.'

'Your mother was here again this morning.'

'Was she really?'

'You wouldn't see her. Again.'

'Last time she was here I saw her.'

'You attacked her, Rebi. You became violent. You didn't recover for two days. Why were you so angry? Don't you think you could reach an accommodation with her?'

Bobby, Bobby, I'm still here. I'm still your girl, Bobby.

'No, I don't think so.'

'But she wants very much to reconcile with you. And since your father's death you're all she has in the world. Won't you even let her try?'

Bobby, help me, Bobby. I don't know how much of this bitch I can take!

'Rebi? Rebi? Are you still here?'

'I'd see my father if he came to visit. I love the old fool, I guess.'

'But, Rebi, your father — '

'He loves me, too. I can tell. Poor guy doesn't have a clue, the way that bitch leads him around by the nose, but he loves me. He does. She doesn't love anybody except herself.'

'But Rebi, you know that your father is dead. You're all that your mother has and

344

she's all that you have. If you would reconcile with her, I really think it would help you make progress. You want to go home, don't you? Back to your home and back to your school? If you tested clean for thirty days, I would be able to sign you out for a visit with your mother. Eventually, release you to her custody. I'm sure you'd want that, Rebi.'

'I need some meds, Doctor. I'd be all right if I had some meds. I know I would.'

'No, you wouldn't, Rebi. It was meds that got you in trouble. Do you remember what your life was like before you came to us?'

'I was having fun. I was married, do you know that? I had a good husband and he loved me. I want to get back with him. You can't keep me here. I'm not a criminal.'

'No, you're not, Rebi. You're not a criminal and you're not married. You're a young girl who's been very, very sick. I'm trying to help you, Rebi, but I can't help if you won't let me.'

'How about a couple of jellybeans?'

'No jellybeans, Rebi. You know how

much harm those pills cause.'

Bobby would give me jellybeans.

'Rebi, I have to show you something.' Dr. Takakura produced a file folder from someplace, Red couldn't tell where it came from. The doctor opened the folder and took a sheet of paper from it and laid it on the table between them. She pointed at a line of figures on the paper. 'Do you see those numbers, Rebi? Those are the results of your latest urine test.'

'Yeah, right. Don't you have enough of your own? What do you need mine for?'

'You know why we need your urine, Rebi. It tells us whether you've been using again. And you have.'

'Sorry 'bout that.'

'How do you get them, Rebi? How do you get drugs, here of all places?'

'Oh, Doctor, I don't know what you're talking about. I don't use drugs anymore. You and your fine staff have shown me the error of my ways.' She held up her fingers in a mock Girl Scout salute. 'How does the saying go? No, wait, don't tell me, I've got it memorized. I learned it in one of those stupid schools they sent me to.' She stood up and closed her eyes and recited, 'Mens sana in corpore sano. There, I got it right, didn't I?'

'All right, Rebi. I'm sorry. The deputy will be here in a few minutes to take you back to your room. We'll try again in a couple of days.'

Dr. Takakura left the faux living room. From Rebi's side the door looked like an ordinary room door with an ordinary doorknob, but she could hear the click as Dr. Takakura left. She knew that the door could only be opened with a key, and she didn't have one. She didn't have one yet.

Red walked over to the window and stood watching the traffic passing on the distant freeway. She took her hair in her two fists. Her hair was growing in once more, actually getting pretty long again. She pulled it with both hands. It made her head feel funny when she did that. It wasn't quite a jolt but it helped. And she knew, she knew, she knew she could get something. You can always get something. Anywhere.

There was that deputy who liked girls, especially young, skinny girls.

Red smiled to herself. Yes. You could always get something.

Isn't that so, Bobby? Isn't that so?

Other titles in the
Linford Mystery Library:

BLING-BLING, YOU'RE DEAD!

Geraldine Ryan

When the manager of newly-formed girl band Bling-Bling needs a Surveillance Operator to protect them, retired policeman Bill Muir jumps at the chance — but he doesn't know what he's let himself in for . . . In *Making Changes*, Tania Harkness is on a mission to turn around her run-down estate. But someone else is equally determined to stop her . . . And in *Another Country*, Shona Graham returns to her native Orkney island of Hundsay to put right a wrong that saw her brother ostracised by the community many years previously . . .

THE DOPPELGÄNGER DEATHS

Edmund Glasby

While investigating a fatal car crash, Detective Inspector Vaughn's interest is piqued when forensic evidence points to murder, and he is shown the eerie antique doll found sitting on the passenger seat. The blood-spattered doll bears an extraordinary resemblance to the dead man, and on its lap is an envelope containing the message: 'One down. Five to go.' When a second doll is discovered beside another murder victim, the desperate race is then on to find and stop the killer from completing the set of six murders . . .

THE OTHER FRANK

Tony Gleeson

When Detective Frank Vandegraf hears of the unexpected death of his ex-wife, he travels to the tiny rural town of Easton to face the demons of his past. But it's no respite from the challenging urban crimes of his regular job. No sooner has he arrived than two bizarre, violent deaths occur, and he feels irresistibly drawn to help unravel a web of mystery and intrigue. However, he's out of his jurisdiction, obstructed by officials, and amidst folk hiding their own secrets . . .

LEGACIES

Steven Fox

Following in the footsteps of Sherlock Holmes and Doctor John Watson come their twenty-first-century descendants, Sergeant Samuel Holmes and Doctor Jamesina Watson, great-grandchildren of their famous forebears, working for the London, California police force. In their first case together, the pair must investigate a series of mysterious murders where the bodies of the victims are apparently unmarked. In doing so, they uncover a sinister conspiracy from a very old enemy that threatens not only their own lives, but those of their families . . .

A FROZEN SILENCE

Arlette Lees

Deputies Frack Tilsley and Robely Danner are called to a remote section of woods outside their small farming community of Abundance, Wisconsin, where a man stands handcuffed and frozen to a tree. As they investigate this brutal murder, a young woman discovers the purse of a missing secretary from nearby Promontory which contains a cryptic diary. Digging deeper, Tilsley and Danner discover common denominators linking several suspects to two murder victims and possibly a third, with the chief of police himself on their list . . .